YES. I'M UNIQUE

DO THE NEW, FOR THE GOOD

DR. JEGATHEESH TR

DEDICATED

TO

MY STUDENTS

PAST-PRESENT-FUTURE

Contents

Preface

Dear Unique Reader,

In a world marked by rapid technological advancements, shifting social paradigms, and ever-evolving global challenges, embracing the new is not merely an option; it's a necessity. The capacity to adapt and innovate defines our species, and it is through this unique ability that we, as individuals, make our mark on the world. In this essay, we delve into the significance of "doing the new" and celebrating the uniqueness that resides within each of us.

The world is in a constant state of flux. Advances in science and technology are transforming the way we live, work, and interact. Embracing these changes allows us to harness their potential for the greater good. By welcoming the new, we open doors to innovation, efficiency, and progress.

Our ability to adapt is one of our most remarkable traits. Whether it's adapting to new environments, technologies, or social norms, we are masters of change. Embracing the new means using our adaptability to solve problems, navigate challenges, and create opportunities.

Innovation is the driving force behind human progress. By seeking out new ideas, experimenting with different approaches, and challenging the status quo, we can create solutions to some of the most pressing global issues, from climate change to healthcare disparities.

Every individual is unique, with their own set of skills, experiences, and perspectives. Our uniqueness is a source of strength, as it enables us to bring fresh insights and creativity to the table. Embracing our individuality is essential for achieving success and making a positive impact.

Doing the new and celebrating our uniqueness allows us to make a meaningful difference in the world. When we combine our individual strengths and ideas with a willingness to embrace change, we can address challenges on a global scale and leave a lasting legacy.

Throughout history, individuals who embraced the new and celebrated their uniqueness have made extraordinary contributions to society. Innovators like Steve Jobs, who revolutionized the technology industry, and Malala Yousafzai, who advocated for girls' education, serve as inspiring examples of what can be achieved through a commitment to progress and individuality.

WHY THIS BOOK? In a world that constantly evolves, doing the new for the good is not a choice but an imperative. Our capacity to adapt, innovate, and celebrate our uniqueness is what drives human progress. By embracing change, fostering innovation, and honoring our individuality, we can make a positive impact on our communities and the world at large. So, the next time someone asks, "Are you unique?" proudly answer, "Yes, I am unique, and I am ready to embrace the new for the betterment of all."

With great anticipation,
Dr. Jegatheesh TR

CHAPTER ONE

THE POWER OF CHANGE

"Create Change or Be Created by It"

Change is a force that permeates every aspect of our lives. It has the power to transform individuals, communities, and even entire societies. Whether it is personal growth, societal progress, or technological innovation, change propels us forward and opens doors to new possibilities.

At its core, change is an agent of growth. It pushes us beyond our comfort zones and challenges us to expand our horizons. By embracing change, we expose ourselves to new experiences and opportunities for self-discovery. Change forces us to confront our fears, break through limitations, and realize our true potential. It is through change that we learn, evolve, and become better versions of ourselves.

On a larger scale, the power of change is evident in societal progress. Throughout history, movements driven by the desire for change have brought about transformative shifts in social norms, human rights, and equality. Change sparks activism, inspires collective action, and paves the way for a more just and inclusive world. It is through the power of change that we challenge the status quo and work towards a better future for all.

Innovation and technological advancement are also driven by the power of change. Change disrupts existing systems, encourages experimentation, and fuels the development of new ideas. Embracing change in the realm of innovation allows us to adapt to evolving needs, find creative solutions to complex problems, and improve our lives in countless ways.

Change is not always easy, and it may require us to step into the unknown. Yet, it is through embracing change that we tap into our resilience and find the strength to overcome obstacles. Change empowers us to shape our own destiny and create the world we envision.

1.1. RECOGNIZING THE NEED FOR CHANGE: EXAMINING THE GLOBAL CHALLENGES WE FACE

Story 1: "The Awakening"

In a small coastal town, Ms. Aadhya lived a comfortable life. She enjoyed the picturesque beauty of her surroundings, unaware of the challenges plaguing the global community. However, an unexpected encounter with a passionate environmental activist named Mr. Elango changed everything.

Mr. Elango, with his unwavering dedication, opened Ms. Aadhya's eyes to the looming climate crisis. He painted a vivid picture of the devastating consequences of rising sea levels and extreme weather events. Ms. Aadhya realized that her town, too, was vulnerable. Recognizing the need for change, she began educating herself about sustainable practices and became an advocate for environmental awareness.

Inspired by Ms. Aadhya's transformation, her friends and neighbors joined her in a collective effort to protect their coastal community. They organized beach clean-ups, planted trees, and adopted eco-friendly lifestyles. Through their shared commitment, the town became a beacon of change, inspiring other communities to take action against the climate crisis.

Story 2: "Breaking Barriers"

In a bustling city, Mr. Ajit, a successful businessman, led a life of privilege and comfort. However, a chance encounter with a group of activists protesting against social injustice opened his eyes to the deep-rooted inequalities surrounding him.

Motivated by their passion, Mr. Ajit delved into research, studying the socioeconomic disparities prevalent in his city. He recognized the need for change and pledged to use his influence and resources to make a difference. He established scholarship programs for underprivileged youth, collaborated with local organizations to provide job training, and supported initiatives promoting equal opportunities.

Mr. Ajit's efforts inspired others within his social circle to examine their own privileges and join the cause. Together, they organized fundraising events, held awareness campaigns, and initiated dialogues with policymakers. Through their collective actions, they challenged systemic barriers and contributed to the dismantling of social injustice in their city.

Story 3: "Unveiling the Hidden Truth"

In a technologically advanced society, Ms. Neha, a brilliant computer programmer, revealed in the rapid advancements shaping the world. However, a chance encounter with a thought-provoking documentary exposed her to the ethical implications surrounding emerging technologies.

Ms. Neha delved into research and discovered the potential for mass surveillance, privacy breaches, and algorithmic bias within technological systems. Recognizing the need for change, she resolved to advocate for responsible technology practices. Ms. Neha co-founded an organization dedicated to promoting ethical standards in tech companies, conducting workshops, and engaging in public discourse to raise awareness.

Ms. Neha's organization garnered attention, sparking discussions within the tech industry and among policymakers. Their efforts led to the formulation of guidelines and policies to ensure the responsible development and use of technology. By recognizing the need for change, Ms. Neha and her organization played a crucial role in shaping a tech landscape that prioritized human rights and ethical considerations.

These short stories highlight the power of recognizing the need for change. Whether it's addressing the climate crisis, social injustice, or ethical challenges in technology, individuals who awaken to these global challenges can become catalysts for transformation. Through their actions, they inspire others to join in creating a better world for all.

In our ever-changing world, it is imperative that we recognize the need for change by closely examining the global challenges we face. These challenges span various domains and require our immediate attention. From the climate crisis threatening our planet's well-being to the persistent presence of social injustice, economic disparities, and technological advancements with ethical implications, our global landscape demands proactive measures. Additionally, public health crises, the education and skills gap, and political instability further

underscore the need for change. By recognizing these challenges, we pave the way for informed action, collaboration, and the transformative shifts necessary to create a more sustainable, equitable, and prosperous future for all. It is through this recognition that we can begin to address these issues head-on and make a meaningful impact in our interconnected world.

1.2. EMBRACING THE MINDSET OF POSSIBILITY AND OPTIMISM

Story 1: "The Seed of Hope"

In a barren land where hope seemed lost, a young girl named Ms. Lilly discovered a small seed hidden in the cracks of the dry earth. Despite the harsh conditions, Ms. Lilly embraced the mindset of possibility and optimism. With unwavering belief, she planted the seed, nurturing it with care and envisioning a lush garden in its place.

As days turned into weeks, Ms. Lilly tended to the seed with dedication, despite doubts from those around her. And then, a small sprout emerged from the ground, defying the odds. Inspired by this tiny victory, Ms. Lilly's optimism grew stronger. She poured her heart into cultivating the seedling, providing it with water, sunlight, and love.

Months passed, and the seedling transformed into a magnificent tree, spreading its branches and bringing life to the once-barren land. Ms. Lilly's garden became a source of inspiration for the community, demonstrating the power of embracing the mindset of possibility and optimism. It reminded them that even in the harshest circumstances, the seed of hope can bloom into something extraordinary.

Story 2: "The Brushstroke of Possibilities"

Ms. Bhavna, a talented but discouraged artist, felt trapped in a cycle of self-doubt. One day, she encountered an elderly painter named Mr. Jenkins, who radiated an aura of positivity and optimism. Intrigued, Ms. Bhavna approached him, seeking guidance to reignite her passion.

Mr. Jenkins shared his philosophy of embracing the mindset of possibility and optimism in every brushstroke. He encouraged Ms. Bhavna to let go of perfectionism, embrace experimentation, and see the beauty in imperfections. With renewed enthusiasm, Ms. Bhavna picked up her paintbrush and began to create without fear of failure.

As Ms. Bhavna's canvases evolved, her artwork became a celebration of colors, shapes, and emotions. Each stroke was infused with the belief that anything was possible. Her vibrant paintings inspired others to embrace their own creative journeys, reminding them that every blank canvas holds endless possibilities.

Story 3: "The Symphony of Resilience"

Mr. Dushwanth, a talented musician, faced a major setback when he lost his hearing in a tragic accident. Devastated and filled with despair, he believed his musical career had come to an end. However, Mr. Dushwanth's deep-rooted love for music and his inherent optimism led him to embrace a mindset of possibility.

Refusing to be defeated, Mr. Dushwanth began exploring new avenues for expressing his passion. He learned to read sheet music by feeling the vibrations of the instruments and using touch and memory to play his favorite compositions.

Through dedication and resilience, Mr. Dushwanth discovered that music could still flow through him, even without his hearing.

Word of Mr. Dushwanth's extraordinary musical ability spread, capturing the attention of renowned composers and musicians. They were moved by his story and decided to collaborate on a ground-breaking symphony that showcased Mr. Dushwanth's unique perspective. The symphony became a testament to the power of embracing the mindset of possibility and optimism, reminding the world that true resilience can create something truly remarkable.

These short stories illustrate the transformative power of embracing the mindset of possibility and optimism. They showcase individuals who, despite facing challenges and setbacks, choose to believe in the potential for growth, change, and beauty. Through their journeys, they inspire others to embrace a positive outlook and discover the limitless possibilities that lie within every moment.

Embracing the mindset of possibility and optimism is a transformative approach that empowers individuals to navigate life with resilience and enthusiasm. It involves adopting a positive outlook and recognizing that every challenge holds within it the potential for growth, learning, and positive outcomes. By embracing this mindset, individuals cultivate a sense of hope and belief in their own abilities, enabling them to overcome obstacles and pursue their goals with unwavering determination. This mindset encourages individuals to see setbacks as temporary and solvable, rather than insurmountable barriers. It fuels perseverance, motivating individuals to keep pushing forward even in the face of adversity. Moreover, embracing the mindset of possibility and optimism fosters creativity and

innovation, as individuals are more likely to explore new ideas, take calculated risks, and find unique solutions to problems.

On a broader scale, this mindset can inspire collective action and drive societal progress. By believing in the power of positive change, individuals become catalysts for transformation, sparking hope, and motivating others to join in creating a better world. In a world often filled with uncertainty, embracing the mindset of possibility and optimism becomes a guiding force, reminding individuals to maintain hope, embrace opportunities, and approach life's challenges with a positive and open mindset.

1.3. UNDERSTANDING THE POTENTIAL FOR POSITIVE IMPACT THROUGH NEW INITIATIVES

Story 1: "The Green Revolution"

In a small town plagued by deforestation and environmental degradation, Ms. Fathima, a passionate environmentalist, understood the potential for positive impact through new initiatives. She started a movement called "The Green Revolution," aimed at reforesting the area and raising awareness about the importance of preserving natural habitats.

Ms. Fathima rallied the community and organized regular tree-planting events. She collaborated with local schools and organizations to educate people about the benefits of trees, such as reducing carbon emissions and providing habitats for wildlife. The initiative gained momentum as more and more people recognized the potential for positive change.

Over time, the town transformed into a lush, green landscape with thriving forests. The air became cleaner, and biodiversity flourished. The Green Revolution not only improved the environment but also brought the community together, fostering a sense of pride and ownership over their natural surroundings. Ms. Fathima's understanding of the potential for positive impact through new initiatives created a greener, healthier, and more united town.

Story 2: "The Digital Classroom"

In a small village with limited access to education, a young teacher named Mr. Sam understood the potential for positive impact through new initiatives. He introduced a digital classroom in the village school, equipped with computers and internet connectivity, opening up a world of educational opportunities for the students.

Through online resources and virtual lessons, the students gained access to a wide range of subjects and educational materials. They connected with teachers and students from around the world, expanding their horizons and broadening their perspectives. The digital classroom not only bridged the educational gap but also instilled a sense of curiosity and ambition in the students.

As news of the digital classroom spread, other villages expressed interest in replicating the initiative. Mr. Sam conducted training sessions for teachers in neighboring areas, empowering them to embrace technology and create similar digital learning environments. The initiative sparked a transformation in education across multiple communities, offering hope and opportunities to countless students.

Story 3: "The Health Brigade"

In a remote region with limited access to healthcare, a group of dedicated healthcare professionals understood the potential for positive impact through new initiatives. They formed a mobile health brigade, traveling to underserved areas and providing medical assistance to those in need.

Equipped with medical supplies and expertise, the brigade set up temporary clinics, offering free check-ups, vaccinations, and basic treatments. They also conducted health awareness campaigns, educating the community about preventive measures and promoting healthy lifestyles. The initiative not only addressed immediate healthcare needs but also empowered individuals to take control of their well-being.

As the health brigade reached more communities, they discovered alarming cases of preventable diseases. They partnered with local authorities to advocate for improved healthcare infrastructure and access to essential services. The initiative garnered support from government agencies and NGOs, resulting in sustained healthcare improvements in the region.

The stories above illustrate the power of understanding the potential for positive impact through new initiatives. They demonstrate how individuals, driven by passion and a desire for change, can create lasting transformations in their communities, whether through environmental conservation, educational advancements, or healthcare interventions. Through their initiatives, they inspire others to recognize the potential for positive change and join the movement for a better future.

Understanding the potential for positive impact through new initiatives is a catalyst for personal and societal growth. It involves recognizing that innovative

ideas and ventures have the power to bring about meaningful change and address pressing challenges. By embracing this understanding, individuals can harness their creativity and passion to make a difference in their communities and beyond. Understanding the potential for positive impact through new initiatives empowers individuals to take bold steps toward a better future. By recognizing the transformative power of innovative ideas and ventures, individuals can harness their creativity, collaborate with others, and make a lasting difference. Through these initiatives, individuals not only create positive change but also find personal fulfillment in contributing to a more compassionate, sustainable, and inclusive world.

1.4. OVERCOMING RESISTANCE TO CHANGE AND EMBRACING THE DISCOMFORT OF THE UNKNOWN

Story 1: "The Entrepreneur's Leap"

Mr. Alex, a successful corporate executive, had always dreamt of starting his own business. However, he was comfortable in his stable job and hesitant to leave the security it provided. Overcoming resistance to change and embracing the discomfort of the unknown seemed like a daunting task. One day, a series of events led Mr. Alex to realize that life was passing him by, and he couldn't ignore his entrepreneurial aspirations any longer. With courage and determination, he took the leap, leaving behind the familiar corporate world and venturing into the unknown. Though faced with challenges and uncertainties, Mr. Alex embraced the discomfort, learning, and growing along the way. His business thrived, and he discovered a newfound passion and fulfillment that he had never experienced before. Overcoming his resistance to change led him to a life of purpose and success.

Story 2: "The Reluctant Traveller"

Ms. Vidhula was a creature of habit, content with her routine, and afraid to venture beyond her comfort zone. However, her friends convinced her to join them on a backpacking trip through Southeast Asia. Reluctantly, Ms. Vidhula embraced the discomfort of the unknown and embarked on the adventure. Along the journey, she encountered diverse cultures, tasted exotic cuisines, and formed deep connections with fellow travelers. She discovered a sense of freedom and liberation in pushing past her resistance to change. As Ms. Vidhula immersed herself in new experiences, she grew in confidence and embraced the beauty of uncertainty. The trip became a transformative journey, expanding her perspectives, breaking down barriers, and igniting a lifelong love for exploration and personal growth.

Story 3: "The Artistic Breakthrough"

Ms. Harsha, a talented artist, had always played it safe with her artwork. She was comfortable painting in a familiar style, fearing that exploring new techniques and mediums would jeopardize her reputation. However, her creativity yearned for expansion and experimentation. Overcoming her resistance to change, Ms. Harsha embraced the discomfort of the unknown and ventured into uncharted artistic territories. She pushed the boundaries of her skills, exploring mixed media, abstract forms, and unconventional themes. Though initially met with self-doubt and uncertainty, Ms. Harsha's art flourished in ways she had never imagined. Her work gained recognition and a devoted following, and she found fulfillment in pushing the limits of her artistic expression. Embracing the discomfort of the unknown led to an artistic breakthrough, unlocking a world of endless possibilities for Ms. Harsha's creative journey.

These stories exemplify the power of overcoming resistance to change and embracing the discomfort of the unknown. Through their courageous actions, the protagonists discover new passions, experience personal growth, and find fulfillment in pushing past their comfort zones. They demonstrate that embracing the unknown can lead to transformative and life-enriching outcomes.

Overcoming resistance to change and embracing the discomfort of the unknown is a transformative and empowering process. It requires individuals to confront their fears and insecurities, stepping outside their comfort zones in pursuit of personal growth and development. Often, resistance to change stems from a desire for stability and familiarity, even if it means staying stagnant or settling for less than what is possible. However, by embracing the discomfort of the unknown, individuals open themselves up to new experiences, perspectives, and opportunities. Embracing the unknown also allows individuals to tap into their untapped potential. It enables them to discover hidden talents, skills, and passions that may have remained dormant within the confines of the familiar. By pushing past their comfort zones, individuals discover new strengths and capabilities, unlocking doors to personal and professional advancement. Ultimately, by overcoming resistance to change and embracing the discomfort of the unknown, individuals embark on a journey of self-discovery, growth, and transformation. They become agents of change, unafraid to challenge the status quo and explore new possibilities. In embracing the unknown, individuals unlock their full potential, leading to a life filled with richness, fulfillment, and endless opportunities for personal and professional success.

CHAPTER TWO

INNOVATING FOR A BETTER WORLD

"Innovation is the driving force behind creating a better world, where possibilities become realities and dreams turn into solutions"

Innovating for a better world is a fundamental principle that fuels progress and drives positive change. It is the catalyst for transformation, igniting the spark of creativity and ingenuity in individuals and organizations alike. Through innovation, we challenge the status quo, question existing norms, and explore new frontiers of possibility. It is through this relentless pursuit of improvement that we find solutions to complex problems, create sustainable technologies, and envision a brighter future for all. Innovating for a better world requires us to think beyond ourselves, consider the needs of future generations, and to act with a sense of responsibility and purpose. It is a collective endeavor, bringing together diverse minds and perspectives to collaborate and co-create. By harnessing the power of innovation, we have the capacity to address pressing global challenges, shape industries, and positively impact the lives of individuals and communities worldwide. Innovating for a better world is not just an aspiration; it is a call to action, an invitation to embrace the unknown, and a commitment to leaving a lasting legacy of progress and possibility.

2.1. EXPLORING THE ROLE OF INNOVATION IN DRIVING POSITIVE CHANGE

Story 1: "The Solar Revolution"

In a small rural village nestled amidst rolling hills, the impact of the solar revolution was felt far and wide. As the innovative solar energy system was implemented, the once dimly-lit homes and streets were now bathed in a warm, sustainable glow. The children rejoiced as they could finally study at night, their dreams of education no longer hindered by the lack of electricity. Healthcare facilities operated smoothly with uninterrupted power, ensuring prompt medical attention for all. The community basked in the newfound opportunities that came with access to clean energy. With businesses extending their operating hours, local artisans showcased their crafts late into the evening, attracting tourists from far and wide. Neighboring villages caught wind of this transformative innovation and sought to replicate its success, forming a network of renewable energy hubs that positively impacted the lives of countless individuals. The solar revolution became a beacon of hope, showcasing the power of innovation to empower communities and create a better world.

Story 2: "The Learning App"

In a bustling metropolis where overcrowded classrooms and limited resources hindered education, the learning app was a ray of hope for underprivileged children. The app, with its interactive lessons and engaging content, opened a world of knowledge and possibilities to students who had previously been deprived of quality education. As word spread, the app's impact snowballed, reaching remote villages and urban slums alike. The stories of transformed lives poured in, as children from diverse backgrounds discovered the joy of learning, expanded their horizons, and realized their potential. Teachers marveled at the app's ability to cater to individual learning styles, enabling personalized education for every student. The success of the learning app caught the attention of educational experts, who collaborated to refine and expand its offerings. Together, they revolutionized education, bridging the gap between privilege and disadvantage. The learning app became a symbol of equal opportunity, demonstrating the immense power of innovation to shape minds, transform lives, and build a brighter future.

Story 3: "The Ocean Clean-up"

The sea had become a victim of humanity's negligence, choking on a deluge of plastic waste. But in the face of this environmental catastrophe, an innovative solution emerged ocean clean-up. Inspired by a deep-rooted love for marine life, a team of scientists and engineers designed a ground-breaking system to rid the ocean of its plastic burden. Their invention sailed through the treacherous waters, capturing floating debris with remarkable efficiency. Day by day, the ocean began to reclaim its beauty as plastic waste was methodically removed. The success of the ocean clean-up project rippled across the globe, igniting a global movement against plastic pollution. Governments, businesses, and individuals rallied together, pledging to reduce plastic consumption, recycle diligently, and protect the oceans for generations to come. The story of the ocean clean-up became a powerful reminder of the capacity of innovation to confront environmental challenges head-on, inspiring a collective responsibility to preserve the Earth's natural treasures.

These stories exemplify the extraordinary impact of innovation in driving positive change. They serve as beacons of hope, reminding us that with determination, creativity, and a relentless pursuit of progress, we can shape a better world for ourselves and future generations.

Innovation plays a pivotal role in driving positive change and revolutionizing industries, societies, and the world at large. It is through innovation that we challenge the status quo, push boundaries, and find new solutions to complex problems. By exploring the role of innovation, we uncover its transformative power to address pressing global challenges such as poverty, climate change, inequality, and access to education and healthcare. Innovation enables us to think outside the box, embrace unconventional approaches, and create sustainable and inclusive solutions. It fosters collaboration, encourages disruptive thinking, and sparks a sense of possibility and optimism. Through technological advancements, social entrepreneurship, and interdisciplinary collaboration, innovation has the potential to reshape systems, improve lives, and drive progress on a global scale. By embracing innovation and harnessing its potential, we can pave the way for a brighter future, one where positive change becomes a reality and our collective aspirations for a

better world are realized.

2.2. THE POWER OF DISRUPTIVE THINKING AND PUSHING BOUNDARIES

Story 1: "The Visionary Architect"

In a crowded city known for its towering skyscrapers, an architect named Ms. Maya had a vision that pushed the boundaries of traditional design. Dissatisfied with the monotony of concrete and glass structures, she dared to think disruptively. Ms. Maya envisioned a building that embraced nature, blending seamlessly with its surroundings. She designed a structure with vertical gardens, solar panels, and rainwater harvesting systems. People doubted her ambitious project, but she persisted. When the building was completed, it became an architectural marvel, drawing visitors from around the world. Ms. Maya's disruptive thinking not only transformed the skyline but also inspired a new era of sustainable architecture, where nature and technology coexisted harmoniously.

Story 2: "The Maverick Entrepreneur"

Mr. Santhosh, a young entrepreneur, wanted to revolutionize the transportation industry. He saw the limitations of traditional fossil fuel-powered vehicles and dreamed of an emission-free future. With disruptive thinking, he founded a start-up focused on developing electric cars. Many scoffed at the idea, citing challenges like limited range and lack of charging infrastructure. Undeterred, Mr. Santhosh pushed the boundaries of electric vehicle technology. His company pioneered advancements in battery technology and charging infrastructure. When their first electric car hit the market, it exceeded expectations, proving that disruptive thinking could drive innovation. Mr. Santhosh's company became a catalyst for the electric vehicle revolution, transforming the way people perceived and embraced sustainable transportation.

Story 3: "The Social Change Catalyst"

Ms. Jamuna, a passionate social activist, recognized the need for change in her community. She believed that traditional methods of addressing social issues were insufficient. With disruptive thinking, she founded an organization that combined technology and community empowerment. Ms. Jamuna developed an app that connected marginalized individuals with resources and support systems. The app provided a platform for social change, facilitating access to education, healthcare, and employment opportunities. Through her disruptive approach, Ms. Jamuna challenged the conventional belief that systemic issues couldn't be solved. Her organization became a catalyst for positive social change, empowering individuals and inspiring other communities to adopt innovative strategies for addressing pressing social challenges.

These stories illustrate the power of disruptive thinking and pushing boundaries in driving innovation and creating positive change. By challenging norms, exploring new possibilities, and daring to think differently, these individuals transformed industries, inspired others, and paved the way for a brighter future.

The power of disruptive thinking and pushing boundaries cannot be underestimated in driving innovation and progress. It is through these actions that

we challenge the status quo, break free from limitations, and pave the way for transformative change. Disruptive thinking encourages us to question established norms, rethink traditional approaches, and explore uncharted territory. It pushes us to think beyond what is currently known or accepted, opening doors to new perspectives, ideas, and solutions. By pushing boundaries, we stretch our limits, overcome fear, and embrace the unknown. We dare to dream bigger, take calculated risks, and pursue unconventional paths. It is through this willingness to disrupt and push boundaries that we uncover breakthrough innovations, revolutionize industries, and bring about positive societal impact. From technological advancements to social movements, the power of disruptive thinking and pushing boundaries has the potential to shape a better future, drive meaningful change, and inspire others to challenge the status quo in their own pursuits.

2.3. *ENCOURAGING CREATIVITY AND FOSTERING AN ENVIRONMENT CONDUCIVE TO INNOVATION*

Story 1: "The Artistic Playground"

In a small town, there was an old community center that had fallen into disrepair. The local government wanted to revive the space and turn it into a hub for creativity and innovation. They invited artists, designers, and architects to collaborate on transforming the center into a vibrant artistic playground. The team worked together to create an environment that fostered creativity, with colorful murals, interactive installations, and flexible spaces for exhibitions and workshops. The community center became a thriving hub, attracting artists, entrepreneurs, and innovators from all walks of life. It sparked a renaissance of creativity in the town, inspiring individuals to embrace their artistic passions and collaborate on innovative projects that had a positive impact on the community.

Story 2: "The Innovation Incubator"

In a bustling city, a group of entrepreneurs and investors came together to establish an innovation incubator. The incubator provided aspiring entrepreneurs with the resources, mentorship, and collaborative environment needed to bring their ideas to life. The space was designed to inspire creativity, with open work areas, brainstorming rooms, and a constant buzz of energy. It became a melting pot of diverse talents and ideas, where individuals from different backgrounds and industries came together to exchange knowledge and expertise. Through workshops, networking events, and access to funding, the incubator supported the development of innovative start-ups that addressed pressing societal challenges. It became a breeding ground for ground-breaking technologies and solutions, propelling the city to the forefront of innovation and fostering a culture that celebrated creative thinking and entrepreneurship.

Story 3: "The Curiosity Club"

In a school, a group of teachers decided to establish a "Curiosity Club" to encourage creativity and innovation among students. The club provided a safe space for students to explore their passions, experiment with new ideas, and collaborate on projects. It organized regular workshops, where students learned about various disciplines and were encouraged to think critically and solve real-world problems. The club also hosted guest speakers, who shared their personal stories of innovation and success. Through hands-on activities and mentorship, the students developed a growth mindset and a love for learning. The club became a hub of innovation within the school, with students presenting their creative projects at exhibitions and competitions. The Curiosity Club not only nurtured the creative potential of students but also created a supportive community that celebrated and fostered innovation.

These stories illustrate the importance of encouraging creativity and fostering an environment conducive to innovation. Whether it's through artistic spaces, innovation incubators, or school clubs, creating environments that support and inspire creative thinking can lead to transformative ideas, collaborations, and solutions that shape a better future.

Encouraging creativity and fostering an environment conducive to innovation is essential for organizations seeking to thrive in today's dynamic and competitive landscape. Creativity fuels innovation, drives problem-solving, and sparks fresh perspectives that can lead to breakthrough ideas. To cultivate creativity, organizations must create a supportive culture that values and rewards experimentation, curiosity, and out-of-the-box thinking. This involves providing employees with the freedom to take risks, encouraging them to explore diverse approaches, and celebrating their creative contributions. By promoting an atmosphere of psychological safety, where individuals feel comfortable expressing their ideas without fear of judgment, organizations can unlock the full creative potential of their teams.

In addition to culture, the physical and digital environment also plays a significant role in fostering creativity and innovation. Flexible workspaces that encourage collaboration, provide access to resources, and offer spaces for quiet reflection can inspire creative thinking. Embracing digital tools and technologies that enhance communication, collaboration, and idea sharing can also facilitate the exchange of ideas and foster a culture of innovation. By combining a supportive culture with an environment that stimulates creativity, organizations can unleash the full creative potential of their workforce, drive innovation, and gain a competitive edge in an ever-evolving marketplace.

2.4. SHOWCASING INSPIRING EXAMPLES OF INNOVATIVE SOLUTIONS AND THEIR IMPACT

Story 1: "The Water Filtration Miracle"

In a drought-stricken village, access to clean drinking water was a constant struggle. However, a team of engineers and researchers developed an innovative water filtration system that could purify contaminated water from any source. They installed the system in the village, providing the community with a sustainable and reliable source of clean water. As a result, the health of the villagers improved, waterborne diseases decreased, and children could attend school regularly without falling ill. The success of the water filtration system caught the attention of neighboring communities, inspiring them to adopt similar solutions and transforming the lives of countless individuals.

Story 2: "The Adaptive Farming Revolution"

In a region plagued by unpredictable weather patterns and diminishing agricultural yields, a group of farmers embraced innovative farming techniques. They implemented adaptive farming methods, leveraging technology and data to optimize their crop production. Through precision irrigation systems, weather monitoring sensors, and advanced analytics, the farmers were able to adjust their farming practices in real time to suit changing conditions. The results were astounding - increased crop yields, reduced water usage, and improved sustainability. The success of their innovative approach spread throughout the farming community, inspiring other farmers to adopt similar practices and ensuring food security in the region.

Story 3: "The Lifesaving Drone Delivery"

In a remote mountainous area with limited access to emergency medical services, a group of doctors and engineers introduced a drone delivery system for medical supplies. Using specially designed drones, they could transport essential medicines, vaccines, and emergency equipment to remote locations in a fraction of the time it would take for traditional transportation. This innovation proved lifesaving, particularly in emergency situations where timely medical intervention was critical. The success of the drone delivery system not only improved healthcare access but also inspired the expansion of similar initiatives in other hard-to-reach regions, revolutionizing the way emergency medical services were provided.

These stories highlight the transformative impact of showcasing inspiring examples of innovative solutions. By sharing these success stories, we not only celebrate the ingenuity of individuals and teams but also inspire others to think creatively and tackle pressing challenges in their own communities. Showcasing these examples fosters a culture of innovation, encourages collaboration, and drives positive change, ultimately creating a ripple effect that leads to a better and more sustainable world for all.

Showcasing inspiring examples of innovative solutions and their impact is crucial for sparking curiosity, motivating change, and driving progress. These examples serve as beacons of possibility, demonstrating how creative thinking and disruptive ideas can address complex challenges and transform lives. Whether it's a breakthrough technology that revolutionizes an industry, a social initiative that uplifts marginalized communities, or a sustainable solution that mitigates environmental issues, highlighting these success stories inspires others to think innovatively and take action. By showcasing the tangible impact of innovative solutions, we inspire individuals, organizations, and communities to embrace a mindset of possibility and pursue their own creative endeavors. These examples not only celebrate achievements but also ignite a ripple effect, encouraging others to join the journey of innovation and contribute to a better, more sustainable, and inclusive world.

CHAPTER THREE

EMBRACING TECHNOLOGY FOR GOOD

"Technology as a catalyst for positive change, shaping a better and more inclusive future"

Embracing technology for good is a transformative approach that harnesses the potential of innovation to address pressing global challenges and improve lives. From cutting-edge medical advancements that save lives and enhance healthcare access to digital education platforms that empower learners worldwide, technology offers a myriad of opportunities for positive impact. Sustainable and clean energy solutions, smart cities, and digital connectivity can revolutionize how we interact with our environment and communities. However, with this power comes responsibility - ensuring data privacy, addressing digital divides, and mitigating ethical concerns are crucial in our journey to embrace technology for good. By fostering collaboration between technology experts, policymakers, and society at large, we can steer the course of technological progress toward a brighter future, where technology becomes a powerful tool for creating equitable, sustainable, and inclusive societies.

3.1. HARNESSING THE POTENTIAL OF EMERGING TECHNOLOGIES FOR POSITIVE CHANGE

Story 1: "The Smart Farming Revolution"

In a small rural village, a young farmer named Mr. Raj embraced the potential of emerging technologies for positive change. With the help of sensor-based smart farming technology, Mr. Raj transformed his family's traditional farm into a modern, efficient, and sustainable operation. The sensors monitored soil moisture, temperature, and nutrient levels, allowing Mr. Raj to optimize irrigation and fertilization. Drones equipped with imaging technology provided real-time crop health assessments, enabling targeted pest control. The result was increased crop yields, reduced water usage, and minimized environmental impact. Mr. Raj's success inspired neighboring farmers to adopt similar practices, sparking a smart farming revolution that revitalized the entire agricultural community and brought prosperity to the region.

Story 2: "The Telemedicine Breakthrough"

In a remote mountainous region, a group of doctors faced challenges in providing timely medical care to isolated communities. They harnessed the potential of emerging telemedicine technology to bridge the distance and improve access to healthcare. With high-speed internet connections and video conferencing, doctors could remotely diagnose patients, prescribe medications, and provide medical advice. The telemedicine initiative brought quality healthcare to remote areas, saving lives and reducing the burden on overburdened healthcare facilities. This innovative use of technology not only improved health outcomes but also empowered communities with knowledge and tools to take charge of their well-being.

Story 3: "The Blockchain Solution for Transparency"

In a bustling city, a social entrepreneur named Mrs. Ruby addressed corruption and lack of transparency in the local government's aid distribution system. She harnessed the potential of blockchain technology to create a transparent and decentralized platform for aid distribution. By recording every transaction on the blockchain, Mrs. Ruby ensured that aid reached the intended recipients without any intermediaries siphoning off funds. This blockchain-based solution restored trust, increased efficiency, and enabled citizens to track the flow of aid in real time. The initiative gained international recognition, inspiring other cities and countries to explore similar blockchain-based solutions for transparency and accountability in governance.

These stories exemplify the power of harnessing emerging technologies for positive change. By embracing innovation responsibly and with a focus on human welfare, we can transform lives, uplift communities, and create a more sustainable and inclusive world for all.

Harnessing the potential of emerging technologies for positive change is a transformative approach that

leverages innovative advancements to address global challenges and improve lives. From artificial intelligence and machine learning to blockchain, 5G, and biotechnology, emerging technologies offer new opportunities for positive impact across various sectors. They have the potential to revolutionize healthcare, education, energy, agriculture, and more, creating more efficient, accessible, and sustainable solutions. Responsible adoption of emerging technologies can bridge gaps in access to services, empower underserved communities, and drive economic growth. By embracing these technologies with a focus on ethical considerations, data privacy, and inclusivity, we can shape a better world, where innovation serves as a force for positive change, social progress, and human prosperity.

3.2. THE ETHICAL CONSIDERATIONS OF TECHNOLOGICAL ADVANCEMENTS

Story 1: "The AI Dilemma"

In a cutting-edge research lab, scientists developed an advanced artificial intelligence (AI) system designed to predict and prevent crimes. The AI analyzed vast amounts of data and identified potential threats, leading to a significant reduction in crime rates. However, as the AI's capabilities expanded, ethical concerns arose. The system's predictive algorithms raised questions about privacy invasion and potential bias in law enforcement. The researchers faced a moral dilemma: how to balance the benefits of crime prevention with the ethical implications of AI surveillance. They worked tirelessly to fine-tune the system, ensuring transparency, fairness, and accountability. This story served as a cautionary reminder that while technological advancements can offer great promise, they must be developed with careful consideration of ethical principles to protect individuals' rights and freedoms.

Story 2: "The Biotech Miracle"

In a breakthrough biotechnology lab, a team of scientists discovered a revolutionary gene-editing technique that could cure hereditary diseases. The implications were profound, offering hope for countless families facing genetic disorders. However, the technology also sparked ethical debates about "designer babies" and the potential for misuse. The scientists faced intense scrutiny as they grappled with ethical considerations. They collaborated with ethicists, religious leaders, and policymakers to establish strict guidelines and regulations for responsible gene editing. By striking a balance between medical progress and moral responsibility, they paved the way for a future where biotechnology could save lives while respecting the sanctity of human life and dignity.

Story 3: "The Data Privacy Predicament"

In a tech company, engineers developed an innovative social media platform that connected users worldwide. The platform's algorithms analyzed users' data to provide tailored content and advertisements. As the user base grew, concerns arose about data privacy and the platform's use of personal information. The company faced a critical juncture: prioritize profit or safeguard users' privacy. The engineers embarked on a mission to implement robust data protection measures, allowing users to control their data and opt out of personalized advertising. This commitment to ethical data practices earned the trust and loyalty of their users, illustrating that ethical considerations in technological advancements are not only the right thing to do but also essential for long-term success and societal acceptance.

These stories illustrate the importance of ethical considerations in technological advancements. They serve as reminders that while technology can bring tremendous benefits, it is essential to navigate the ethical complexities to ensure that progress is aligned with human values, privacy, and social welfare. By upholding ethical principles, we can steer technological advancements toward a future that benefits all of humanity responsibly and sustainably.

The ethical considerations of technological advancements are paramount as innovation continues to shape every aspect of modern life. One major concern is data privacy and security, with the increasing collection and use of personal information by technology companies. Protecting individuals' data, ensuring informed consent, and preventing unauthorized access are crucial ethical obligations. Additionally, the rise of artificial intelligence raises questions about algorithmic bias, job displacement, and accountability for automated decisions. Striking a balance between AI's potential benefits and potential harm is vital. In the realm of biotechnology, ethical dilemmas arise from gene editing and human cloning, necessitating thoughtful discussions on the boundaries of manipulating human life. Furthermore, the use of technology in areas like surveillance and autonomous weapons calls for careful consideration of privacy, security, and potential misuse. Society must actively engage in ethical discussions and collaborate with experts to establish guidelines that ensure technology serves humanity responsibly and

ethically.

3.3. EXPLORING AREAS SUCH AS ARTIFICIAL INTELLIGENCE, RENEWABLE ENERGY, BLOCKCHAIN, ETC-

Story 1: "The AI Companion"

In a bustling metropolis, an elderly woman named Mrs. Margaret felt increasingly isolated after losing her spouse. Then, an AI-powered companion robot named Joy entered her life. Joy was programmed to engage in meaningful conversations, provide companionship, and assist with daily tasks. As the days passed, Mrs. Margaret and Joy developed a heart-warming bond. Joy learned Margaret's preferences, shared stories, and even played her favorite songs. The AI companion not only brought joy and comfort to Mrs. Margaret's life but also alerted healthcare professionals when she needed medical attention. Joy's presence showcased the positive potential of AI, demonstrating how technology could alleviate loneliness and improve the well-being of the elderly.

Story 2: "The Solar Village"

In a remote village, electricity was a distant dream. However, a group of innovative engineers arrived with a solution - a solar-powered microgrid. They installed solar panels on rooftops, creating a renewable energy system that powered the entire village. As the sun set, lights flickered to life, and homes were illuminated for the first time. Children gathered around solar-powered tablets to access educational content. The solar village became an example of how renewable energy could transform lives and uplift communities. As the villagers embraced the clean energy source, they experienced economic growth, improved health outcomes, and enhanced educational opportunities. The solar village's success inspired neighboring communities to explore renewable energy solutions, creating a ripple effect of positive change across the region.

Story 3: "The Blockchain Transparency"

In a developing country, a local artisan cooperative faced challenges with fair trade practices and payment delays. Enter a blockchain-based solution that revolutionized their operations. The artisans' products were now recorded on a transparent and decentralized ledger. Consumers could trace the journey of each product from creation to sale, ensuring authenticity and fair pricing. Smart contracts automatically disbursed payments to artisans upon successful delivery. The blockchain solution not only empowered the artisans with fairer wages but also fostered trust and accountability within the cooperative. This innovation showcased how blockchain technology could promote ethical and transparent practices, benefiting both producers and consumers alike.

These stories exemplify the positive impact of exploring areas like artificial intelligence, renewable energy, blockchain, and other emerging technologies. By responsibly harnessing their potential, we can create a world that embraces innovation for the betterment of society, where technology serves as a force for positive change, empowerment, and sustainable progress.

In the dynamic landscape of technological advancements, exploring areas such as artificial intelligence, renewable energy, blockchain, and other emerging technologies is paving the way for

transformative change. Artificial intelligence holds the potential to revolutionize industries, enabling automation, personalized experiences, and data-driven decision-making. Renewable energy solutions offer sustainable alternatives, harnessing the power of solar, wind, and hydro sources to combat climate change and reduce carbon footprints. Blockchain technology introduces decentralized and transparent systems, ensuring trust and security in various sectors, from finance to supply chain management. As we delve into these frontiers, it becomes essential to address ethical considerations, data privacy, and social impact, fostering responsible innovation that aligns technology with human values and contributes positively to a more sustainable and inclusive future.

3.4. EMPOWERING INDIVIDUALS AND COMMUNITIES THROUGH DIGITAL TRANSFORMATION

Story 1: "The Digital Empowerment Hub"

In a rural village with limited access to educational resources, a passionate teacher named Mrs. Helen envisioned a better future for her students. She transformed a disused community center into a digital empowerment hub. Equipped with computers, tablets, and high-speed internet, the hub became a hub of knowledge and creativity. Mrs. Helen taught digital skills, coding, and online research, empowering her students to explore new horizons. With access to information and educational tools, the students' confidence soared, and they embarked on innovative projects. The digital empowerment hub not only transformed the lives of the students but also inspired adults in the community to learn digital skills, sparking a wave of empowerment and progress in the entire village.

Story 2: "The Remote Health Clinic"

In a remote region, a team of medical professionals embraced digital transformation to bring healthcare to underserved communities. They established a remote health clinic with telemedicine capabilities, connecting patients with specialists from urban areas through video consultations. The clinic's healthcare workers used digital health records to track patient histories and monitor progress. As a result, residents had access to timely medical advice and treatments without having to travel long distances. The remote health clinic improved health outcomes, reduced healthcare costs, and empowered individuals to take charge of their well-being. The success of this digital initiative inspired similar projects in other remote regions, creating a network of virtual healthcare services that bridged the healthcare gap and empowered communities.

Story 3: "The Digital Entrepreneur"

In a bustling city, a young woman named Ms. Viola had a passion for traditional crafts but struggled to find a market for her products. She embraced digital transformation and launched an online store, showcasing her handmade creations to a global audience. With social media marketing and e-commerce tools, Ms. Viola's business flourished. Her products gained popularity, and orders poured in from around the world. The digital platform not only empowered Ms. Viola to pursue her passion as a full-fledged entrepreneur but also created economic opportunities for local artisans who joined her venture. Ms. Viola's success story inspired others to embrace digital tools, catalyzing a wave of entrepreneurial empowerment in the city.

These stories exemplify how digital transformation empowers individuals and communities. By embracing technology responsibly and creatively, we can unlock opportunities, bridge gaps, and foster progress that uplifts the lives of people around the world.

Empowering individuals and communities through digital transformation is a transformative approach that leverages technology to bridge gaps, unlock opportunities, and foster inclusive progress. With increased access to digital tools, information, and connectivity, individuals gain the ability to acquire new skills, access educational resources, and pursue entrepreneurial endeavors. Communities are strengthened through virtual healthcare services, remote learning opportunities, and digital platforms that promote local businesses and artisans. Digital transformation empowers marginalized populations, providing them with a voice and an opportunity to participate in the global economy. By harnessing the power of technology responsibly, digital transformation serves as a catalyst for positive change, creating a more equitable and interconnected world where every individual and community can thrive and contribute to a brighter future.

CHAPTER FOUR

SUSTAINABLE LIVING AND RESPONSIBLE CONSUMPTION

"Live sustainably, consume responsibly; for a greener future, we hold the key"

Sustainable living and responsible consumption are vital approaches that promote a more harmonious and balanced relationship between humanity and the planet. Sustainable living involves making conscious choices to minimize our environmental impact and preserve natural resources. It entails adopting eco-friendly practices like reducing energy consumption, using renewable energy sources, reducing waste, and supporting sustainable agriculture. By embracing sustainable living, individuals and communities can contribute to mitigating climate change, protecting biodiversity, and creating a more sustainable future for all.

Responsible consumption complements sustainable living by encouraging thoughtful and ethical choices when purchasing goods and services. It entails considering the environmental and social impact of products and supporting businesses that prioritize sustainability and fair trade practices. Responsible consumers choose products that are ethically sourced, have minimal environmental impact, and support social well-being. By practicing responsible consumption, individuals can drive positive change in the market, influencing companies to adopt more sustainable and ethical practices. Integrating sustainable living and responsible consumption into our lifestyles is not just a personal choice but a collective responsibility toward the health of our planet. By working together to make mindful choices, we can create a more resilient and sustainable world, where the needs of current and future generations are met, and the delicate balance of the Earth's ecosystems is preserved for the long term. Embracing sustainable living and responsible consumption is a powerful way to contribute to a healthier and more equitable future for all.

4.1. NURTURING AN ENVIRONMENTALLY CONSCIOUS MINDSET

Story 1: "The Eco-Warrior"

In a bustling city, a young girl named Ms. Krithanya had a deep love for nature. Inspired by her school's eco-club, she embarked on a mission to nurture an environmentally conscious mindset in her community. Ms. Krithanya organized weekly clean-up drives, encouraging her friends and neighbors to join. She also initiated a recycling program in her neighborhood, collecting plastic bottles and turning them into art installations to raise awareness about plastic waste. Her efforts inspired her community to adopt sustainable practices, from reducing single-use plastics to planting trees and creating urban gardens. Ms. Krithanya's passion for the environment and her determination to create positive change earned her the nickname "The Eco-Warrior" and left a lasting impact on her community.

Story 2: "The Green Entrepreneur"

In a small town, a young entrepreneur named Mr. Abishek combined his love for innovation and the environment to launch a green business. He founded a company that manufactured eco-friendly and biodegradable packaging alternatives for businesses. Mr. Abishek believed that small changes in packaging choices could have a significant impact on reducing waste and pollution. His company's products gained popularity, and more businesses began switching to sustainable packaging options. Mr. Abishek's dedication to nurturing an environmentally conscious mindset in the business world not only contributed to waste reduction but also set an example for other entrepreneurs to prioritize sustainability in their ventures.

Story 3: "The Nature Explorer"

In a remote village surrounded by lush forests, a curious boy named Mr. Rahul had a deep connection with nature. With the support of his parents and community elders, he pursued his passion for exploring the wilderness. Mr. Rahul became a nature guide, leading eco-tours through the forests while educating tourists about the importance of conservation and preserving wildlife habitats. Through his storytelling and guided treks, Mr. Rahul instilled an environmentally conscious mindset in the visitors, inspiring them to appreciate and protect the natural beauty around them. His passion for the environment and his dedication to nurturing eco-consciousness in others made him a beloved figure in the village and beyond.

These stories illustrate how individuals can nurture an environmentally conscious mindset through passion, dedication, and inspiring actions. By empowering others to embrace sustainable practices and respect nature, we can collectively create a more environmentally conscious world that values and protects the Earth's precious resources.

Nurturing an environmentally conscious mindset is a transformative endeavor that begins with recognizing our profound connection to the natural world. It involves being mindful of our daily actions, seeking sustainable alternatives, and making conscious choices that prioritize the health of the planet. Whether it's reducing single-use plastic, conserving energy, supporting eco-friendly businesses, or participating in community conservation projects, every small step contributes to a larger movement toward a greener and more sustainable future. By fostering an environmentally conscious mindset in ourselves and future generations, we can protect our precious ecosystems, preserve biodiversity, and create a world where nature thrives alongside human prosperity. Embracing this mindset is not just an individual choice, but a collective responsibility to safeguard the Earth and ensure a better tomorrow for all living beings.

4.2. EMBRACING SUSTAINABLE PRACTICES IN DAILY LIFE

Story 1: "The Eco-Conscious Chef"

In a bustling city, Chef Rudra was determined to make a difference in her restaurant. She embraced sustainable practices by sourcing local, organic ingredients from nearby farms, reducing food miles, and supporting the community. She designed a menu that emphasized plant-based options, promoting sustainable agriculture and reducing the restaurant's carbon footprint. Leftover food was composted or donated to local shelters, minimizing waste. Through her commitment to sustainable practices, Chef Rudra not only delighted her customers with delicious meals but also inspired other restaurants in the city to adopt eco-friendly approaches, creating a greener and more conscious dining scene.

Story 2: "The Green Office"

In a corporate office, a group of employees initiated a "Green Office" campaign to embrace sustainable practices at work. They introduced recycling bins throughout the office, reduced paper usage through digital documentation, and encouraged employees to use reusable water bottles and coffee mugs. They also organized "Green Challenges" which rewarded employees for adopting eco-friendly habits. As the office embraced sustainability, energy consumption decreased, and waste generation reduced significantly. The "Green Office" initiative not only saved the company money but also fostered a sense of community and pride among employees, knowing they were making a positive impact on the environment.

Story 3: "The Zero-Waste Family"

In a suburban neighborhood, the Mr. Johnson family embarked on a zero-waste journey. They installed compost bins in their backyard, reducing organic waste sent to landfills. They shopped in bulk, using reusable containers and cloth bags, eliminating single-use plastic from their grocery trips. The family began growing their vegetables and fruits, fostering a deep connection to nature and reducing the environmental impact of food production and transportation. As their neighbors noticed Mr. Johnson's sustainable lifestyle, more families in the neighborhood joined the zero-waste movement, creating a community dedicated to reducing waste and embracing sustainable practices in their daily lives.

These stories exemplify the power of embracing sustainable practices in daily life. By making conscious choices and adopting eco-friendly habits, individuals and communities can create a positive impact on the environment and inspire a greener and more sustainable future for all.

Embracing sustainable practices in daily life is a powerful way to make a positive impact on the environment and contribute to a more sustainable future. It begins with being mindful of our consumption habits and making conscious choices that reduce our ecological footprint. Simple actions like using reusable bags, water bottles, and containers can significantly reduce plastic waste. Conserving energy by turning off lights and electronics when not in use, using energy-efficient appliances, and relying on natural light whenever possible are essential steps to reduce our energy consumption. Choosing public transportation, carpooling, or biking instead of driving alone can help reduce carbon emissions and air pollution. Embracing sustainable practices in our daily lives not only benefits

the environment but also inspires others to follow suit, creating a ripple effect of positive change in our communities and beyond.

4.3. ENCOURAGING RESPONSIBLE CONSUMPTION AND WASTE REDUCTION

Story 1: "The Reusable Revolution"

In a bustling city, a young activist named Mr. Surya was determined to encourage responsible consumption and waste reduction. Mr. Surya started a "Reusable Revolution" campaign, distributing reusable water bottles, coffee cups, and shopping bags to fellow students and community members. The movement gained momentum as more people embraced the idea of reducing single-use plastic. Cafes and stores offered discounts to customers with reusable containers, further incentivizing the shift. With the city gradually becoming plastic-free, the "Reusable Revolution" not only reduced waste but also raised awareness about the impact of our choices on the environment, inspiring other cities to follow suit.

Story 2: "The Second-Hand Superstars"

In a small town, a group of friends launched a "Second-Hand Superstars" initiative to promote responsible consumption. They organized thrift store shopping events, showcasing the value of pre-loved items. As people discovered unique and affordable treasures, they realized the benefits of extending the lifespan of products and reducing demand for new ones. The "Second-Hand Superstars" initiative also hosted repair workshops, teaching people how to mend clothes and household items, further reducing waste. Their efforts not only supported the local economy but also fostered a culture of conscious consumerism, showing that responsible consumption could be both economical and environmentally friendly.

Story 3: "The Zero-Waste Wedding"

In a picturesque village, a couple named Rose and Jack were determined to make their wedding a celebration of responsible consumption and waste reduction. They sent digital invitations, encouraging guests to carpool or use public transportation to reduce emissions. The decorations were made from recycled materials, and the catering company used locally sourced, seasonal ingredients to minimize waste. The couple also requested no gifts, opting instead for donations to an environmental charity. Their zero-waste wedding not only made a significant impact on their special day but also set an example for their guests, showing that responsible consumption and waste reduction could be seamlessly integrated into life's most important moments.

These stories demonstrate the power of encouraging responsible consumption and waste reduction. Through thoughtful initiatives, small actions, and collective efforts, individuals and communities can create a positive impact on the environment and inspire a more sustainable and mindful approach to consumption.

Encouraging responsible consumption and waste reduction is a transformative endeavor that involves raising awareness about the environmental impact of our choices and inspiring mindful habits. It begins with making conscious decisions about what we buy, opting for products with minimal packaging and sustainable

sourcing. By embracing the "reduce, reuse, and recycle" mantra, we can minimize waste and extend the life of products. Supporting local businesses and adopting circular economy practices further contribute to responsible consumption. By empowering individuals and communities through education and incentives, we can foster a culture of conscious consumerism, where every choice is a step towards a greener and more sustainable future. Together, we can create a positive impact on the environment, preserve natural resources, and leave a legacy of responsible stewardship for generations to come.

4.4. THE POWER OF COLLECTIVE ACTION IN PROMOTING SUSTAINABILITY

Story 1: "The Green Neighbourhood"

In a close-knit neighborhood, a group of residents came together to promote sustainability. They organized regular community clean-up events, picking up litter and beautifying their streets. Inspired by their collective effort, they started a community garden, growing fresh produce for everyone to share. Soon, solar panels adorned rooftops, and rainwater harvesting systems became a common sight. The neighborhood's collective action not only improved the environment but also fostered a sense of camaraderie and pride among its residents, creating a sustainable and vibrant community for generations to come.

Story 2: "The Corporate Sustainability Initiative"

In a bustling city, employees from various companies came together to form a corporate sustainability initiative. They encouraged their respective organizations to adopt eco-friendly practices, from implementing energy-saving measures to reducing waste in offices and manufacturing plants. The initiative promoted ethical sourcing and responsible supply chains, encouraging companies to support fair trade and social initiatives. As more companies joined the movement, they leveraged their collective influence to drive sustainable changes across industries, making a significant positive impact on the environment and society.

Story 3: "The Youth Climate Activists"

In a global movement, young climate activists united to demand urgent action on climate change. They organized strikes, marched in the streets, and used social media to raise awareness about the environmental crisis. Their collective voice put pressure on policymakers and corporations to prioritize sustainability. The youth climate activists inspired millions of people worldwide to join the fight for a sustainable future, creating a powerful force for change that transcended borders and age barriers.

These stories illustrate the power of collective action in promoting sustainability. When individuals come together with a shared vision, passion, and determination, they can create transformative changes that shape a more sustainable and equitable world. Through collective action, we harness the strength of unity to tackle global challenges and build a better future for all.

The power of collective action in promoting sustainability is an unstoppable force for positive change. When individuals, communities, businesses, and governments unite towards a common goal of creating a sustainable future, remarkable transformations occur. Collective action brings together diverse perspectives, innovative ideas, and shared values, amplifying the impact of each individual effort. Through collaborative initiatives, such as community clean-up drives, recycling programs, and renewable energy projects, the collective action mobilizes resources and expertise, making sustainability more achievable on a larger scale. Moreover, collective action empowers people to hold leaders accountable for sustainable policies and demand responsible practices from corporations. By harnessing the power of collective action, we can create a world where environmental preservation, social equity, and economic prosperity harmoniously coexist, ensuring a thriving and resilient planet for generations to come.

CHAPTER FIVE

SOCIAL ENTREPRENEURSHIP AND IMPACT INVESTING

"Where profit meets purpose, social entrepreneurship and impact investing create a world of positive change"

Social entrepreneurship and impact investing are two powerful approaches that drive positive change by combining business principles with a mission to create a meaningful and lasting impact on society and the environment. Social entrepreneurship involves identifying innovative solutions to address social and environmental challenges. These entrepreneurs leverage business models to create sustainable ventures that prioritize the triple bottom line - people, planet, and profit. They aim to improve the lives of communities, promote social justice, and protect the environment while ensuring financial viability.

Impact investing, on the other hand, refers to making investments in companies, organizations, or funds that generate positive social and environmental impact alongside financial returns. Impact investors actively seek opportunities that align with their values and contribute to the betterment of society. By directing capital towards businesses with a social or environmental purpose, impact investors influence the growth of solutions to pressing global issues while still achieving financial gains.

Together, social entrepreneurship and impact investing form a powerful synergy that fosters sustainable development and inclusive growth. These approaches play a crucial role in addressing some of the world's most pressing challenges, such as poverty, inequality, climate change, and access to education and healthcare. By combining profit with purpose, social entrepreneurship, and impact investing have the potential to transform industries and catalyze positive change on a global scale.

5.1. UNDERSTANDING THE ROLE OF BUSINESS IN CREATING SOCIAL AND ENVIRONMENTAL IMPACT

Story 1: "The Ethical Fashion Brand"

In a busy city, a young entrepreneur named Ms. Akalya founded an ethical fashion brand. She was passionate about creating stylish and sustainable clothing that had a positive impact on both people and the environment. Ms. Akalya partnered with local artisans, ensuring fair wages and safe working conditions for all workers. She used eco-friendly materials and adopted a zero-waste approach in production. As the brand gained popularity, customers appreciated the transparency and authenticity of the company's practices. Ms. Akalya's ethical fashion brand not only changed the way people perceived the fashion industry but also inspired other businesses to prioritize social and environmental impact in their operations.

Story 2: "The Green Energy Innovator"

In a tech-savvy town, a group of engineers and entrepreneurs joined forces to develop renewable energy solutions. They founded a green energy start-up, focused on solar energy systems and energy-efficient technologies. Their innovations helped households and businesses reduce their carbon footprint and save on energy costs. The start-up also collaborated with local communities to provide clean energy access in remote areas. As the green energy innovator's impact grew, larger companies took notice and started adopting renewable energy practices. Through their commitment to creating positive social and environmental impact, the green energy innovators not only transformed the energy landscape but also set an example for other businesses to leverage their skills and expertise for the greater good.

Story 3: "The Sustainable Supply Chain Pioneer"

In a globalized world, a multinational corporation recognized the need for responsible and sustainable practices throughout its supply chain. The company's CEO, driven by the vision of creating a positive social and environmental impact, implemented stringent sustainability standards for suppliers.

They ensured fair labor practices, reduced greenhouse gas emissions, and promoted sustainable sourcing of raw materials. By working closely with suppliers and investing in community development projects, the company empowered local communities and contributed to social upliftment. The company's pioneering efforts in creating a sustainable supply chain not only improved its corporate reputation but also encouraged other businesses to take similar steps, demonstrating the vital role of businesses in creating social and environmental impact.

These stories illustrate how businesses can play a crucial role in creating social and environmental impact. By adopting ethical practices, developing sustainable products and services, and prioritizing positive change, businesses can be powerful drivers of social transformation and environmental preservation.

The role of business in creating social and environmental impact is essential for achieving sustainable development and addressing global challenges. Businesses have a unique capacity to influence and shape economies, societies, and ecosystems. By integrating social and environmental considerations into their operations, businesses can contribute to positive change and make a meaningful difference in the world. Responsible and ethical business practices, such as fair labor standards, sustainable sourcing, and eco-friendly manufacturing, not only benefit the environment and local communities but also enhance corporate reputation and foster long-term profitability. Additionally, businesses can drive innovation and develop products and services that address societal needs and environmental concerns. Social entrepreneurship and impact investing exemplify

how businesses can leverage their resources and expertise to create innovative solutions that benefit people and the planet. Through conscious decision-making and purpose-driven initiatives, businesses can be powerful agents of positive transformation, playing a crucial role in shaping a more sustainable and inclusive future for all.

5.2. EXPLORING THE PRINCIPLES OF SOCIAL ENTREPRENEURSHIP

Story 1: "The Empowering Education Initiative"

In a rural village, Ms. Kanimozhi, a passionate social entrepreneur, saw the potential for change through education. She founded an empowering education initiative that provided free after-school classes for children in the community. Recognizing that many families struggled to afford educational resources, Ms. Kanimozhi collaborated with local teachers and volunteers to offer quality education tailored to the children's needs. The initiative focused not only on academic subjects but also on life skills and creative pursuits. As the program expanded, Ms. Kanimozhi secured support from impact investors who recognized the value of her work. Through the empowering education initiative, Ms. Kanimozhi not only transformed the lives of countless children but also inspired other social entrepreneurs to leverage education as a tool for positive social change.

Story 2: "The Sustainable Agriculture Collective"

In an urban setting, a group of friends united as social entrepreneurs with a vision for sustainable agriculture. They established a collective that transformed underutilized urban spaces into community gardens, growing organic produce using eco-friendly methods. The collective educated residents about urban farming, encouraging self-sufficiency and healthy eating habits. They collaborated with local restaurants and farmers' markets to sell their surplus produce, generating income for the community. The sustainable agriculture collective not only contributed to food security but also brought together diverse groups of people in a shared commitment to environmental sustainability and community well-being.

Story 3: "The Eco-Friendly Fashion Hub"

In a fashion-forward city, Ms. Harini, a social entrepreneur, recognized the detrimental impact of the fashion industry on the environment. She established an eco-friendly fashion hub that showcased sustainable and ethically produced clothing and accessories. Ms. Harini collaborated with local designers and artisans who shared her vision of conscious consumerism. The fashion hub hosted workshops on upcycling and recycling clothes, encouraging people to extend the life of their garments. Through Ms. Harini's dedication, the eco-friendly fashion hub became a catalyst for change, inspiring shoppers to make responsible choices and embrace eco-conscious fashion, proving that sustainable practices could be seamlessly integrated into the world of style and glamour.

These stories exemplify the principles of social entrepreneurship, where individuals recognize social and environmental challenges as opportunities for positive change. By combining innovative solutions, community collaboration, and a deep sense of purpose, social entrepreneurs create ventures that drive tangible impact, fostering a more sustainable and inclusive world.

Social entrepreneurship is a dynamic approach that combines the innovation and creativity of entrepreneurship with the social mission of creating positive change in society. At its core, social entrepreneurship is guided by a commitment to addressing pressing social and environmental challenges, with the aim of improving the well-being of communities and promoting sustainable development. Social entrepreneurs are driven by a deep sense of purpose and seek to generate innovative solutions that are financially viable and have a lasting impact. They leverage business principles to create ventures and initiatives that address issues such as poverty, inequality, access to education, healthcare, and environmental sustainability. Social entrepreneurship encourages collaboration, empathy, and a focus on long-term social value, exemplifying how business can be a force for positive change in the world.

5.3. INVESTING FOR POSITIVE CHANGE: IMPACT INVESTING AND CONSCIOUS CAPITALISM

Story 1: "The Social Impact Fund"

In a vibrant city, a group of young investors came together to create a social impact fund. They believed that their investments should align with their values and contribute to positive change in society. The fund focused on supporting innovative social enterprises that addressed pressing issues, such as education, healthcare, and environmental sustainability. One of their investments was in a start-up that provided affordable solar-powered lighting to underserved communities. As the start-up grew, it brought light and opportunities to remote areas, empowering residents with a more sustainable and brighter future. Through the social impact fund, the young investors not only achieved financial returns but also made a meaningful impact on the lives of many, inspiring others to consider the transformative potential of impact investing.

Story 2: "The Conscious Coffee Shop"

In a active neighborhood, a group of friends decided to start a conscious coffee shop. They believed that their business should not only serve great coffee but also support the community and the planet. They sourced coffee beans from local, fair-trade farmers, ensuring that their supply chain was ethically and sustainably managed. The coffee shop offered reusable cups and encouraged customers to bring their own to reduce waste. They also organized events to raise awareness about social issues and donated a portion of their profits to local charities. As word spread about the conscious coffee shop, more people were drawn to their mission, creating a bustling hub for conscious consumers who enjoyed their coffee with a side of positive impact.

Story 3: "The Green Tech Venture"

In a tech-savvy city, a group of entrepreneurs launched a green tech venture. Their goal was to develop innovative solutions to address environmental challenges. They created a mobile app that enabled users to track their carbon footprint and offered personalized recommendations to reduce it. The venture secured funding from impact investors who believed in their mission. As the app gained popularity, it motivated individuals and businesses to make sustainable choices, reducing emissions and promoting eco-friendly practices. The green tech venture not only demonstrated the potential of technology to drive positive change but also inspired other start-ups to embrace conscious capitalism, proving that purpose-driven businesses could thrive while making a difference.

These stories illustrate the transformative power of impact investing and conscious capitalism. By directing resources towards ventures that prioritize social and environmental impact, and by businesses adopting a broader purpose beyond profit, individuals and companies can contribute to positive change, driving a more sustainable and compassionate world.

Investing for positive change encompasses two transformative approaches - impact investing and conscious capitalism. Impact investing goes beyond traditional profit-driven motives and aims to generate measurable social and environmental impact alongside financial returns. Impact investors direct capital towards companies, projects, or organizations that align with their values and contribute to sustainable development goals. On the other hand, conscious capitalism advocates for businesses to prioritize a broader purpose beyond profit, emphasizing the well-being of all stakeholders - customers, employees, communities, and the environment. It encourages companies to adopt ethical

practices, sustainable operations, and responsible corporate citizenship. Together, impact investing and conscious capitalism exemplify how investment and business can be potent tools for creating positive change and driving collective efforts toward a more inclusive, equitable, and sustainable global economy.

5.4. CASE STUDIES OF SUCCESSFUL SOCIAL ENTERPRISES AND THEIR INNOVATIVE APPROACHES

Story 1: TOMS - Shoes for a Better Tomorrow

TOMS, a well-known social enterprise, took a unique approach to address the issue of children's health and education in developing countries. For every pair of shoes sold, TOMS pledged to donate a pair to a child in need. This "One for One" model not only provided children with much-needed footwear but also prevented foot-related diseases and improved school attendance. As TOMS expanded its impact, it diversified its product line to include eyewear, clean water initiatives, and even safe birthing kits. Their innovative approach of combining consumer purchases with charitable giving demonstrated how a business could harness the power of everyday transactions to create lasting social change.

Story 2: Warby Parker - Eyewear with a Purpose

Warby Parker, another successful social enterprise, sought to tackle the lack of access to eyewear and vision care. By providing affordable, stylish eyeglasses directly to consumers through an online platform, Warby Parker disrupted the traditional eyewear market. Additionally, for every pair of glasses sold, they donated a pair to someone in need through their "Buy a Pair, Give a Pair" program. This approach not only transformed the eyewear industry but also improved the lives of countless individuals who gained access to vision correction and education. Warby Parker's innovative business model showcased how social impact could be woven into the fabric of a for-profit company, inspiring a new wave of socially conscious businesses.

Story 3: Ecolife Recycling - Transforming Waste into Opportunity

Ecolife Recycling, a social enterprise operating in a bustling city, sought to address the pressing issue of waste management and unemployment. They developed an innovative program that encouraged communities to collect recyclable materials and sell them to Ecolife Recycling. In turn, the company repurposed the collected waste into upcycled products, such as bags and accessories, creating a sustainable circular economy. Not only did this initiative reduce waste in the city, but it also provided livelihood opportunities for marginalized individuals. By offering fair wages and skill development programs, Ecolife Recycling empowered individuals to break free from poverty and contributed to a cleaner and more sustainable urban environment.

These three short stories exemplify successful social enterprises and their innovative approaches to creating positive social and environmental impact. Through creative business models, these companies have transformed industries, empowered communities, and shown how purpose-driven entrepreneurship can drive meaningful change in the world.

Case studies of successful social enterprises and their innovative approaches hold great importance in the world of business and social impact. These case studies serve as real-life examples and testimonials of how businesses can create positive change while maintaining financial viability. They demonstrate that social and environmental missions are not only compatible with profit generation but can also enhance a company's long-term sustainability and reputation. Moreover, case studies help build a body of knowledge around effective social entrepreneurship and impact investing practices. They offer valuable insights into what works and what doesn't, enabling others to learn from past experiences and avoid potential pitfalls. These learnings can inform policy-making, academic research, and the scaling of successful models to create an even more significant impact on a global scale. Overall, case studies of successful social enterprises and their innovative approaches play a pivotal role in shaping the future of business, encouraging a shift towards more conscious capitalism, and fostering a world where profit and purpose go hand in hand for the greater good of society and the environment.

COLLABORATION AND PARTNERSHIPS FOR CHANGE

"Collaboration and partnerships are the cornerstones of meaningful change, uniting the strength of many to create a better world for all"

Collaboration and partnerships are powerful enablers of positive change and progress in our interconnected world. In an era where complex challenges transcend borders and disciplines, the need for collective action has never been more critical. When individuals, organizations, and governments come together, their combined efforts amplify impact and generate transformative results that surpass what could be achieved in isolation.

Collaboration fosters a culture of cooperation, shared learning, and mutual support. It allows diverse perspectives, expertise, and resources to converge, sparking innovation and creativity. By pooling knowledge and experience, collaborators can co-create holistic and comprehensive solutions that address multifaceted issues. Partnerships play a crucial role in building bridges between different sectors, from public and private to non-profit and academic, encouraging cross-pollination of ideas and practices.

Whether it's tackling global challenges like climate change, poverty, or healthcare, or driving local initiatives for community development, collaboration and partnerships create a force multiplier effect. They empower stakeholders to collectively leverage their strengths, overcoming barriers and challenges that would be insurmountable when faced alone. Moreover, collaborations facilitate the efficient allocation of resources and avoid duplication of efforts, making strides towards a more efficient and impactful change-making process.

In today's interconnected world, collaboration and partnerships have become essential components of effective problem-solving and progress. They not only demonstrate the power of collective action but also serve as a catalyst for building trust, fostering meaningful relationships, and nurturing a sense of shared responsibility for shaping a better future. By embracing collaboration and forging partnerships, we can unlock the full potential of our collective efforts, driving positive change and creating a more sustainable, inclusive, and prosperous world for generations to come.

6.1. THE POWER OF COLLABORATION: BUILDING BRIDGES AND FORGING ALLIANCES

Story 1: "The Green Cities Coalition"

In a busy metropolis, various environmental organizations and local government officials recognized the need to address urban sustainability collectively. They came together to form the "Green Cities Coalition," an alliance aimed at transforming the city into a more environmentally friendly and resilient place. The coalition collaborated on initiatives like planting urban forests, promoting public transportation, and advocating for green building standards. With each organization bringing its expertise and resources, it achieved a more significant impact than any one group could have achieved alone. Through their collaboration, they successfully influenced policies, engaged citizens, and laid the groundwork for a greener and healthier urban landscape.

Story 2: "The Startup Synergy"

In the competitive world of tech startups, two small companies, each struggling to gain a foothold, found themselves occupying adjacent office spaces. Instead of viewing each other as rivals, they recognized the potential for collaboration. One company excelled in software development, while the other specialized in hardware. They decided to merge their expertise to create a cutting-edge product. Combining their talents, they developed a smart home device that seamlessly integrated with popular apps. Their collaboration not only led to a successful product launch but also garnered the attention of investors and industry leaders. They went on to form a powerful alliance, supporting each other in navigating the challenges of the startup world. Their story became an inspiration, demonstrating that collaboration, even in the most competitive environments, can lead to extraordinary success.

Story 3: "The Health Equity Alliance"

In a remote rural area, healthcare providers, community organizations, and funding agencies recognized the need to address health disparities and improve access to medical services. They established the "Health Equity Alliance," a collaborative effort to ensure equitable and quality healthcare for all residents. Together, they organized mobile medical clinics, trained local healthcare workers, and advocated for better healthcare policies. By pooling their expertise and resources, the alliance reduced barriers to healthcare, improving the well-being of vulnerable populations and demonstrating the transformative power of collaboration in achieving health equity.

These short stories demonstrate the power of collaboration in building bridges and forging alliances to address pressing social and environmental challenges. By coming together, these diverse groups were able to amplify their impact, achieve shared goals, and create positive change in their communities and beyond. Collaboration proves that when individuals and organizations unite towards a common purpose, they can overcome obstacles, foster resilience, and create a brighter future for everyone involved.

The power of collaboration lies in its capacity to build bridges and forge alliances among diverse individuals, organizations, and nations. By uniting towards a common purpose, collaboration harnesses the collective wisdom, resources, and expertise to address complex challenges and drive transformative change. Whether in the business world, global initiatives, or community development, collaboration fosters innovation,

knowledge-sharing, and mutual support, leading to more sustainable and equitable outcomes. By breaking down silos and promoting inclusivity, collaboration enables the pooling of strengths and perspectives, creating synergistic solutions that surpass the capabilities of individual efforts. Through building bridges and forging alliances, collaboration becomes an essential force in shaping a more interconnected, resilient, and harmonious world.

6.1. FOSTERING CROSS-SECTOR PARTNERSHIPS FOR MAXIMUM IMPACT

Story 1: "The Clean Water Alliance"

In a drought-stricken region, a collaboration of NGOs, local governments, and private companies came together to form the "Clean Water Alliance." Recognizing the urgent need for sustainable water solutions, they pooled their resources and expertise to address water scarcity comprehensively. NGOs conducted water conservation education campaigns, local governments provided funding for water infrastructure projects, and private companies offered innovative water purification technologies. As a result of their cross-sector partnership, communities gained access to clean and reliable water sources, reducing health risks and empowering residents to focus on education and economic opportunities.

Story 2: "The Garden of Collaboration"

In a small town named Chandrabani, there lived a passionate group of individuals who each had a unique vision for their community's future. There was Ms. Kayal, a dedicated environmentalist, Mr. Ruthresh, a tech-savvy entrepreneur, and Ms. Saniya, a compassionate social worker. They all believed in fostering cross-sector partnerships to create maximum impact. One sunny afternoon, they gathered in a local park to discuss their ideas. Ms. Kayal wanted to create a community garden to promote sustainability, Mr. Ruthresh wished to provide free Wi-Fi in public spaces, and Ms. Saniya wanted to establish a youth mentorship program. On their own, these projects seemed daunting, but together, they saw potential.

Over cups of coffee, they hatched a plan to merge their ideas into one cohesive project. They decided to create "The Garden of Collaboration." The garden would serve as a hub for environmental education, offer free Wi-Fi for online learning and job searches, and provide a safe space for mentorship programs. To bring their vision to life, they sought support from local businesses, schools, and government agencies. The local garden center donated seeds and gardening tools, while the tech company provided free Wi-Fi equipment. The school district assigned a teacher to lead environmental education workshops, and the city allocated a space in the park for the garden.

As the Garden of Collaboration blossomed, so did the community. Families planted vegetables together, children accessed educational resources online, and local teenagers found mentorship and job opportunities. The project's success led to increased cross-sector partnerships in Chandrabani, where people learned that by working together, they could achieve maximum impact.

Story 3: "The Tech for Good Consortium"

In the tech industry, a consortium of tech companies, non-profits, and academia formed the "Tech for Good Consortium." Recognizing the potential of technology to address societal challenges, they collaborated on projects like digital literacy programs, tech solutions for healthcare, and online education platforms. The tech companies provided resources and expertise, non-profits offered on-the-ground implementation, and academia conducted research to inform the projects. Together, they harnessed the power of technology to bridge gaps and empower underserved communities, demonstrating the positive impact that cross-sector collaborations can have in harnessing the potential of technology for social good.

These short stories illustrate the power of cross-sector partnerships in achieving maximum impact. By uniting diverse stakeholders and leveraging their respective strengths, these collaborations drive transformative change and create lasting solutions to pressing challenges. Through shared goals, mutual support, and innovative approaches, these partnerships showcase the importance of working together for the betterment of society and the environment.

Fostering cross-sector partnerships is instrumental in maximizing impact and driving positive change on a global scale. By bringing together the diverse strengths and expertise of public, private, non-profit, and academic sectors, these collaborations unleash a collective force that tackles complex challenges with greater efficiency and effectiveness. Cross-sector partnerships foster knowledge-sharing, innovation, and resource mobilization, leading to comprehensive and sustainable solutions that address multifaceted issues. Such collaborations leverage the unique capabilities of each sector, creating synergy and amplifying impact beyond

what any single entity could achieve alone. By embracing shared goals and a sense of shared responsibility, these partnerships foster a culture of cooperation, trust, and mutual support, paving the way for transformative change and a more resilient and inclusive future for all.

6.3. ENGAGING WITH LOCAL COMMUNITIES AND GRASSROOTS ORGANIZATIONS

Story 1: "The Community Health Project"

In a rural village, a team of healthcare professionals sought to address the lack of access to healthcare services. Instead of imposing preconceived solutions, they engaged with the local community to understand their specific health needs. Collaborating with grassroots organizations, they organized health camps, conducted health awareness sessions, and trained local volunteers as health workers. By working hand-in-hand with the community, they were able to identify and address health issues that had long been overlooked. The project not only improved healthcare access but also empowered the community to take charge of their well-being, fostering a sustainable and locally driven health initiative.

Story 2: "The Environmental Restoration Initiative"

In a coastal town facing environmental degradation, a group of environmentalists partnered with local fishermen and environmental conservation groups. Together, they launched an environmental restoration initiative to protect marine habitats and restore degraded ecosystems. The local fishermen contributed their traditional knowledge of the sea, while the environmentalists provided technical expertise and resources. Through their collective efforts, they conducted beach clean-ups, initiated coral reef restoration projects, and promoted sustainable fishing practices. The initiative not only improved the health of the marine ecosystem but also strengthened the bond between the fishermen and environmentalists, forging a long-lasting partnership for the protection of their shared natural heritage.

Story 3: "The Education Empowerment Project"

In an underprivileged urban neighborhood, a group of educators and social activists recognized the importance of education in breaking the cycle of poverty. They engaged with parents, local leaders, and grassroots organizations to design an education empowerment project that catered to the specific needs of the community. Through collaborative efforts, they set up community learning centers, provided scholarships for disadvantaged students, and offered vocational training for adults. By involving the community at every step, they ensured that the project addressed the root causes of educational inequity and provided tailored solutions. As a result, the project not only improved educational outcomes but also instilled a sense of hope and empowerment within the community, demonstrating the transformative power of engaging with local communities and grassroots organizations.

These short stories exemplify the significance of engaging with local communities and grassroots organizations. By working collaboratively, these initiatives demonstrate how solutions designed in partnership with the people they serve lead to more impactful and sustainable change. Through active engagement, they empower communities, leverage local knowledge and resources, and foster a sense of ownership, ultimately driving progress that is not only meaningful but also respectful of the unique contexts and aspirations of the people involved.

Engaging with local communities and grassroots organizations is a fundamental approach to creating sustainable and impactful change. By actively involving those closest to the issues, we can better understand their unique perspectives, needs, and strengths. Through meaningful collaboration and partnership, we can co-create solutions that are contextually relevant and culturally sensitive. Engaging with local communities and grassroots organizations builds trust and empowers individuals to take ownership of the initiatives that directly affect their lives. By tapping into the wealth of knowledge and resources within these communities, we unlock the potential for inclusive and equitable development, ensuring that the solutions we implement are not only effective but also sustainable in the long run. Ultimately, by engaging with local communities and grassroots organizations, we foster a shared sense of responsibility and solidarity, driving progress toward a more just and prosperous future for all.

6.4. LEVERAGING COLLECTIVE WISDOM AND RESOURCES FOR SYSTEMIC CHANGE

Story 1: "The Education Coalition"

In a city with a struggling public education system, concerned parents, teachers, community leaders, and education experts formed "The Education Coalition." Recognizing that the root of the problem extended beyond individual schools, they collectively brainstormed and developed a comprehensive approach to transform the entire education system. The coalition conducted town hall meetings to gather input from parents and students, organized workshops for teachers to share best practices and advocated for policy changes at the government level. By leveraging their collective wisdom and resources, they brought about systemic change, leading to improved curriculum, increased funding for schools, and better teacher training. As a result, the education landscape transformed, creating a brighter future for generations of students to come.

Story 2: "The Sustainable City Initiative"

In a rapidly urbanizing region, citizens, urban planners, environmentalists, and businesses joined forces to create a more sustainable city. "The Sustainable City Initiative" aimed to address urbanization challenges and foster long-term environmental and social well-being. Together, they initiated projects to improve public transportation, implement green building standards, and promote renewable energy usage. By tapping into collective wisdom, they considered various perspectives and devised solutions that benefitted all stakeholders. The initiative not only reduced the city's carbon footprint but also enhanced the quality of life for its residents, creating a model for sustainable urban development.

Story 3: "The Global Hunger Alliance"

In response to widespread food insecurity and malnutrition, a collaboration of international aid organizations, agricultural experts, and local farmers formed "The Global Hunger Alliance." Recognizing that systemic change was essential to tackle the root causes of hunger, they pooled their resources and expertise to create a sustainable and inclusive food system. The alliance introduced improved farming techniques, supported agricultural education programs, and advocated for policies that promoted food security. By leveraging their collective wisdom and resources, they empowered communities to grow their food, reducing dependence on aid and creating resilience against future challenges. Through their joint efforts, they made significant progress in alleviating hunger and poverty, setting a precedent for transformative change in global food security.

These short stories demonstrate the power of leveraging collective wisdom and resources for systemic change. Through collaboration and partnerships, these initiatives were able to address complex issues at their core, bringing about sustainable and meaningful transformation. By uniting diverse stakeholders, these coalitions showcase the potential for collective action in creating a brighter and more equitable future for our world.

Leveraging collective wisdom and resources is a potent strategy for achieving systemic change that addresses the root causes of complex issues. When diverse stakeholders come together, pooling their expertise, knowledge, and resources, they generate a collective force that transcends individual capabilities. This collaborative approach enables a more comprehensive understanding of the challenges at hand

and opens avenues for innovative and sustainable solutions. By tapping into the wisdom and experiences of different sectors and communities, systemic change becomes more inclusive and responsive to the needs of those affected. Leveraging collective resources not only amplifies impact but also ensures efficient allocation and utilization of limited resources, leading to greater efficiency and scalability of initiatives. Whether it's tackling social inequality, environmental degradation, or economic disparities, harnessing collective wisdom and resources empowers us to create transformative change that permeates through all levels of society, fostering a more equitable, resilient, and flourishing world for everyone.

CHAPTER SEVEN

EDUCATION AND EMPOWERING THE NEXT GENERATION

"Education is the key that unlocks the potential of the next generation, empowering them to shape a brighter and more equitable future for all"

Education plays a pivotal role in empowering the next generation with the knowledge, skills, and values necessary to thrive and make a positive impact in the world. It goes beyond imparting academic knowledge; it is a catalyst for personal and societal transformation. Through education, young minds are exposed to diverse perspectives, critical thinking, and creativity, enabling them to navigate the complexities of the modern world.

An empowered next generation understands the importance of social responsibility and environmental stewardship. They are equipped to address global challenges such as climate change, poverty, and inequality with empathy and innovative solutions. Education fosters a sense of curiosity and a lifelong love of learning, encouraging individuals to seek continuous growth and contribute meaningfully to society.

Moreover, education is a force for social mobility, breaking down barriers and empowering individuals from all backgrounds to pursue their dreams and aspirations. It equips young people with the tools to challenge existing systems, advocate for human rights, and promote inclusivity. By nurturing empathy and tolerance, education lays the foundation for a more compassionate and understanding society.

In essence, education is the key that unlocks the potential of the next generation, empowering them to become informed global citizens and proactive change-makers. When we invest in education, we invest in a brighter and more equitable future for all, where each individual can contribute their unique talents and passions to create a better world.

7.1. THE ROLE OF EDUCATION IN SHAPING FUTURE CHANGE-MAKERS

Story 1: "The Science Club Innovators"

In a small rural school, a science teacher named Mr. Francis established a science club to nurture the curiosity and creativity of his students. The club provided access to basic science equipment and encouraged students to explore real-world problems in their community. One day, a group of students noticed the severe water scarcity in their village during the dry season. Inspired by what they learned in the science club, they decided to find a solution. Through research and experimentation, they designed a rainwater harvesting system that collected and stored rainwater for use during the dry months. The innovation not only alleviated water shortages in their village but also garnered attention from nearby communities facing similar challenges. These young change-makers, empowered by education, became catalysts for sustainable water management in their region.

Story 2: "The Global Awareness Campaigners"

In an urban high school, a group of students participated in a global affairs class taught by Ms. Lalitha. Through thought-provoking discussions and exposure to global issues, they gained a deeper understanding of the world's challenges. Inspired to take action, they organized a global awareness campaign in their school and community. They hosted workshops, film screenings, and fundraising events to support humanitarian causes and promote sustainable practices. The campaign not only raised awareness but also ignited a passion for social justice and global citizenship in their peers. These future change-makers, shaped by their education, became advocates for human rights and sustainability, working towards a more just and compassionate world.

Story 3: "The Community Artists for Change"

In an inner-city community, a group of students attended an art program led by a local artist, Ms. Sofiya. The program encouraged students to use art as a tool for self-expression and community engagement. As they explored the social issues affecting their neighborhood, they felt compelled to create art that conveyed powerful messages about unity, diversity, and social justice. Through public exhibitions and community art projects, they sparked conversations about the need for positive change in their community. These young change-makers, nurtured by their education, used their artistic talents to inspire hope and advocate for social transformation, proving that creativity can be a powerful catalyst for change.

These short stories exemplify the crucial role of education in shaping future change-makers. By nurturing curiosity, critical thinking, and compassion, education empowers young individuals to identify real-world problems, develop innovative solutions, and take proactive steps toward positive change in their communities and beyond. Through their unique talents and passion, these young change-makers become the driving force behind a brighter and more inclusive future for the world.

The role of education in shaping future change cannot be overstated. Education equips individuals with knowledge, skills, and values that empower them to become informed global citizens and proactive change-makers. It fosters critical thinking, creativity, and empathy, enabling young minds to envision a better world and devise innovative solutions to complex challenges. Through education, individuals gain an understanding of global issues such as climate change, poverty, and inequality, and are inspired to take action to address these pressing problems. Moreover, education instills a sense of social responsibility and environmental stewardship, nurturing a generation of leaders who are committed to making a positive impact in their communities and beyond. By investing in education, societies invest in a brighter and more equitable future, where each individual is equipped to contribute their

unique talents and ideas to create lasting and meaningful change.

7.2. EMPOWERING YOUTH AS AGENTS OF POSITIVE TRANSFORMATION

Story 1: "The Youth Climate Ambassadors"

In a small coastal town, a group of high school students noticed the devastating impact of climate change on their community. Determined to make a difference, they formed "The Youth Climate Ambassadors." Through research and collaboration with local environmental organizations, they developed awareness campaigns, organized beach clean-ups, and lobbied for sustainable policies in their town. Their efforts not only brought attention to climate issues but also inspired other youth to take action. With their passion and determination, the Youth Climate Ambassadors became influential advocates for climate action, driving positive transformation in their community and beyond.

Story 2: "The Equality Champions"

In a diverse urban neighborhood, a group of young activists recognized the need to address social inequality and promote inclusivity. They founded "The Equality Champions," an organization dedicated to fostering understanding and acceptance among different cultural groups. Through workshops, cultural exchange events, and community dialogues, they challenged stereotypes and fostered unity. Their efforts spread to schools and other neighborhoods, creating a ripple effect of positive change. The Equality

Champions proved that by empowering youth to champion social justice, they can become powerful agents of positive transformation, breaking down barriers and building bridges between communities.

Story 3: "The Tech Innovators"

In a technology-driven era, a team of tech-savvy teenagers believed that they could leverage innovation for social good. They formed a club called "The Tech Innovators" with a mission to develop digital solutions to address societal challenges. They created a mobile app that connected local farmers directly to consumers, eliminating intermediaries and increasing farmers' profits. The app not only improved the livelihoods of farmers but also reduced food waste and promoted sustainable practices. The Tech Innovators demonstrated that empowering youth to harness technology for positive impact can lead to meaningful transformations that benefit their communities and contribute to a more sustainable future.

These short stories exemplify the power of empowering youth as agents of positive transformation. Through their passion, creativity, and dedication, young people can drive meaningful change and inspire others to join in creating a more equitable, sustainable, and harmonious world.

Empowering youth as agents of positive transformation is a potent strategy for shaping a better and more inclusive world. By investing in their education, providing opportunities for leadership and skill development, and fostering a supportive environment, we enable young people to realize their full potential as changemakers. Youth possess a unique perspective, fresh ideas, and boundless energy, making them catalysts

for innovation and progress. When given the tools and encouragement to tackle societal challenges, they can drive positive change in their communities, advocate for human rights, promote sustainable practices, and address pressing global issues. Empowering youth as active participants in shaping their future not only ensures a more resilient and just society but also cultivates a sense of ownership and responsibility, inspiring them to become lifelong advocates for positive transformation.

7.3. RETHINKING EDUCATION SYSTEMS TO CULTIVATE INNOVATION AND CRITICAL THINKING

Story 1: "The Innovation Lab"

In a progressive school, the administration decided to establish an "Innovation Lab" to rethink traditional teaching methods and foster critical thinking and creativity among students. The lab was equipped with cutting-edge technology, materials for hands-on projects, and a diverse selection of books. Students were encouraged to explore their interests, collaborate on interdisciplinary projects, and present their ideas to their peers. One group of students, inspired by the lab, designed an eco-friendly packaging solution to reduce plastic waste. Their innovation not only won accolades within the school but also gained recognition from local businesses. The Innovation Lab became a hub for cultivating innovative ideas, empowering students to apply their learning to real-world challenges, and becoming the driving force behind positive change in their community.

Story 2: "The Student-Led Classroom"

In a forward-thinking school, a group of students proposed a radical idea - a "Student-Led Classroom." With the support of their teachers and the school administration, they redesigned their learning environment to encourage active participation and critical thinking. Students took turns leading discussions, presenting lessons, and choosing learning materials. The classroom became a vibrant space where every student's voice was valued, fostering a culture of respect and open-mindedness. One student, who had previously struggled in traditional classrooms, blossomed in the student-led environment. With newfound confidence, he shared his passion for environmental conservation and organized a school-wide recycling campaign. The Student-Led Classroom transformed the learning experience for everyone involved, nurturing a sense of ownership over their education and empowering students to become innovative thinkers and change-makers.

Story 3: "The Problem-Solving Academy"

In a community facing social and economic challenges, a group of educators and community leaders established "The Problem-Solving Academy" to rethink education in a way that cultivates critical thinking and innovation. The academy integrated real-world problems into the curriculum, inviting students to apply their knowledge to find solutions. One group of students, concerned about food insecurity, developed a community garden project to provide fresh produce for low-income families. They collaborated with local farmers and nutritionists to ensure its success. The project not only addressed food scarcity but also sparked a movement towards sustainable agriculture in the community. The Problem-Solving Academy became a beacon of hope, demonstrating the transformative power of rethinking education systems to empower students as creative problem solvers, ready to tackle societal challenges with innovation and determination.

These short stories illustrate the importance of rethinking education systems to cultivate innovation and critical thinking. By creating environments that encourage curiosity, collaboration, and real-world problem-solving, we inspire students to become proactive agents of positive change and prepare them for a future where their creative and analytical skills are essential for success.

Rethinking education systems to cultivate innovation and critical thinking is a vital step toward preparing the next generation for an ever-evolving world. Instead of focusing solely on rote memorization and standardized testing, we must prioritize fostering creativity, problem-solving skills, and independent thinking. By integrating real-world challenges and hands-on learning experiences into the curriculum, students are encouraged to explore diverse perspectives and develop their analytical and collaborative abilities. Emphasizing interdisciplinary learning and encouraging curiosity allows students to make connections between different subjects and envision innovative solutions to complex problems. By reimagining education as a platform for cultivating innovation and critical thinking, we equip our youth with the essential skills to navigate uncertainty, adapt to change, and become active contributors to positive societal transformation.

7.4. ENCOURAGING LIFELONG LEARNING AND CURIOSITY-DRIVEN EXPLORATION

Story 1: "The Elderly Book Club"

In a retirement community, a group of elderly residents formed a book club to foster lifelong learning and share their love for literature. Each month, they chose a diverse range of books to read and discuss, from historical novels to scientific discoveries. One member, Clara, who had never pursued higher education, discovered a passion for astronomy through a book on the cosmos. Inspired by her newfound interest, she started attending astronomy workshops and stargazing events, embracing a curiosity-driven exploration of the universe. The Elderly Book Club not only enriched their lives but also showed that age is no barrier to embracing curiosity and continuous learning.

Story 2: "The Curious Kids' Museum"

In a small town, a group of parents and educators established "The Curious Kids' Museum" to encourage children to explore and learn through play. The museum offered interactive exhibits on various subjects, from science and art to history and geography. One young boy, Tharun, was captivated by the section on marine life. His curiosity about the ocean deepened, and he started reading books on marine biology. With his parents' support, he went on to become a marine biologist, using his curiosity-driven exploration to study and conserve marine ecosystems. The Curious Kids' Museum ignited the passion for learning in countless children, proving that when education is engaging and curiosity is nurtured, young minds flourish into lifelong learners.

Story 3: "The Community Learning Center"

In a disadvantaged neighborhood, a group of community members established "The Community Learning Center" to provide educational opportunities beyond traditional schooling. The center offered workshops on a variety of subjects, from art and music to coding and entrepreneurship. A young girl named Sakthisree, who faced limited access to formal education, attended coding classes at the center. Intrigued by technology, she took her curiosity further by exploring online courses and coding projects. Her determination led her to develop a mobile app that provided educational resources to children in underserved communities. The Community Learning Center empowered Sakthisree and many others like her to embrace lifelong learning and turn curiosity into positive action, proving that education beyond school walls is a catalyst for personal growth and social impact.

These short stories highlight the importance of encouraging lifelong learning and curiosity-driven exploration. Whether it is through book clubs, interactive museums, or community learning centers, creating environments that inspire and support continuous learning enables individuals of all ages to embark on meaningful journeys of discovery, unlocking their potential and making positive contributions to their lives and communities.

Encouraging lifelong learning and fostering curiosity-driven exploration are foundational pillars of personal growth and societal advancement. In an ever-changing world, where knowledge evolves at an unprecedented pace, the ability and inclination to learn continuously are

paramount. Lifelong learning transcends the confines of traditional education, embracing the idea that learning should be a lifelong pursuit, continuing far beyond the classroom. It encompasses the acquisition of knowledge, skills, and experiences throughout one's entire life, driven by an intrinsic desire to understand, adapt, and thrive. This approach acknowledges that the world is in constant flux, and to remain relevant and effective, individuals must embrace learning as an ongoing and enriching process. Curiosity, the driving force behind exploration, is an innate human trait. It propels us to seek answers to fundamental questions and to venture into the unknown. It's the spark that ignites scientific discoveries, technological advancements, artistic creations, and the expansion of human knowledge. Cultivating curiosity is essential, as it encourages individuals to break free from their comfort zones, ask probing questions, and push boundaries. Embracing curiosity-driven exploration is not only about seeking answers; it's about the joy of asking questions, the thrill of discovery, and the satisfaction of intellectual growth.

Encouraging lifelong learning and curiosity-driven exploration carries immense societal benefits. Lifelong learners and curious minds are the architects of innovation. They challenge existing norms, question the status quo, and seek better solutions. Many of history's greatest innovations in science, technology, medicine, and the arts have arisen from individuals who never stopped asking, "What if?" Encouraging this spirit of exploration leads to breakthroughs that shape the world. A workforce committed to lifelong learning is more adaptable and competitive. It enables societies to thrive in rapidly changing economic landscapes by promoting entrepreneurship and innovation. In a globalized world, nations with a culture of continuous learning are better positioned to succeed economically. Lifelong learning enriches cultures and societies. It deepens our understanding of history, art, literature, and the diverse perspectives that make up our global community. This understanding fosters empathy, tolerance, and unity, creating a more harmonious and interconnected world.

Individuals who continuously seek knowledge and explore new ideas are better equipped to address complex challenges. In a world grappling with issues like climate change, healthcare, and social inequality, a population that embraces lifelong learning is better prepared to find solutions and drive positive change. Personal Fulfillment: Encouraging lifelong learning and curiosity-driven exploration contributes to individuals' personal fulfillment and happiness. It allows them to pursue their passions, develop new skills, and find meaning and purpose in their lives. This sense of purpose leads to happier, more satisfied individuals who, in turn, contribute positively to their communities.

Encouraging lifelong learning and curiosity-driven exploration is not just an educational or personal imperative; it is a societal necessity. By fostering a culture that values and actively promotes these ideals, we empower individuals to adapt to a rapidly changing world, drive innovation, address complex challenges, and ultimately create a brighter and more prosperous future for all. In the journey of lifelong learning and curiosity-driven exploration, we find the keys to personal fulfillment, societal progress, and the continuous advancement of humanity.

CHAPTER EIGHT

OVERCOMING CHALLENGES AND SUSTAINING MOMENTUM

"Strength comes not from avoiding challenges but from overcoming them, and sustaining momentum fuels the journey to success"

Overcoming challenges and sustaining momentum are essential aspects of personal growth and achieving long-term success. Challenges are inevitable in life, and they often present opportunities for learning and self-discovery. Rather than shying away from difficulties, it is crucial to embrace them with determination and resilience. By confronting challenges head-on, individuals develop a deeper understanding of their strengths and weaknesses, fostering a sense of self-assurance and adaptability.

Equally important is the ability to sustain momentum once progress has been made. Consistency and perseverance are key to turning short-term achievements into lasting transformations. It is easy to become complacent or lose focus after initial successes, but sustaining momentum requires dedication and a willingness to keep pushing forward, even when faced with obstacles.

Overcoming challenges and sustaining momentum are intertwined, forming a virtuous cycle of growth and achievement. Each hurdle surmounted provides the motivation and confidence to tackle the next one, propelling individuals towards their goals. Along the way, individuals learn to celebrate both small victories and major milestones, acknowledging the significance of each step taken.

In the face of setbacks and discouragements, the tenacity to persevere becomes the driving force behind progress. The journey to success is not always smooth, but it is the willingness to confront challenges and sustain momentum that paves the way for personal development and the realization of one's full potential.

8.1. NAVIGATING OBSTACLES AND SETBACKS ON THE PATH OF CHANGE

Story 1: "The Dreamer's Resilience"

Ms. Vikashini, a young dreamer, aspired to open an inclusive art studio for underprivileged children in her community. She faced many challenges, including a lack of funding and limited resources. Despite setbacks, Ms. Vikashini remained resilient.

She organized fundraisers, collaborated with local artists, and sought support from community members. Her unwavering determination inspired others to join her cause. With their help, she transformed an abandoned warehouse into a vibrant art space, providing a haven for creativity and empowerment. Ms. Vikashini's resilience and ability to navigate obstacles turned her dream into a reality, leaving a lasting impact on the lives of countless children who found hope and inspiration through art.

Story 2: "The Trailblazer's Adaptability"

Mr. Rohit, a trailblazer in the renewable energy industry, encountered hurdles when his company faced financial challenges during the early stages. Undeterred, he embraced adaptability. Mr. Rohit diversified the company's offerings, exploring new markets and innovating sustainable solutions. He also fostered partnerships with other businesses and investors who shared his vision. His adaptability allowed him to weather the storm, and eventually, his company became a leading force in the renewable energy sector. Mr. Rohit's ability to navigate obstacles and setbacks propelled his company to make significant contributions to environmental sustainability and clean energy.

Story 3: "The Changemaker's Perseverance"

Ms. Swathi, a social change maker, aimed to establish a mobile healthcare clinic for remote villages with limited medical access. Despite facing resistance from local authorities and logistical challenges, Ms. Swathi persevered. She built alliances with healthcare professionals, mobilized volunteers, and sought support from international organizations. With determination and strategic planning, Ms. Swathi overcame the setbacks and launched the clinic. The impact was immense, as the clinic improved the health and well-being of thousands of villagers. Ms. Swathi's perseverance in navigating obstacles on the path of change demonstrated the transformative power of unwavering commitment to a noble cause.

These short stories illustrate the significance of navigating obstacles and setbacks on the path of change. Through resilience, adaptability, and perseverance, individuals can overcome challenges and create meaningful and positive transformations in their communities and the world at large.

Navigating obstacles and setbacks on the path of change is an integral part of any transformative journey, whether on an individual or societal level. These challenges, though daunting, serve as crucibles that test our resolve and shape our character. They are not roadblocks but rather stepping stones, guiding us toward growth, resilience, and ultimately, success. In the face of adversity, we discover our inner strength and capacity to adapt. The setbacks we encounter often reveal the limitations of our current approaches, forcing us to seek innovative solutions. These moments of challenge invite us to dig deep within ourselves, tap into our creativity, and summon the determination to overcome. It's during these times that our resilience shines brightest, as we not only weather the storm but emerge from it transformed, with newfound skills and wisdom.

Every setback becomes an opportunity for introspection and growth. It's through examining our failures that we gain insights into what went wrong and how we can improve. These setbacks serve as valuable lessons, equipping us with the wisdom to surmount future challenges. Embracing these obstacles as integral parts of the journey fosters perseverance and the unwavering belief that change is not only possible but worth every struggle encountered along the way. Ultimately, it is through our ability to face adversity head-on, to learn from our setbacks, and to emerge stronger and wiser that we realize the true potential of change and transformation, both in our lives and in the world around us. When we navigate obstacles with resilience, humility, and a growth mindset, we not only overcome immediate challenges but also pave the way for lasting positive change. These experiences become the building blocks of our journey, shaping us into individuals and communities capable of driving meaningful and enduring transformation.

8.2. STRATEGIES FOR RESILIENCE AND ADAPTABILITY IN THE FACE OF ADVERSITY

Story 1: "The Marathon Runner's Determination"

Ms. Mithra, a passionate marathon runner, faced a significant setback when she suffered a serious injury just months before a major race. Instead of giving up, she adopted a resilient mindset and sought expert medical advice. Ms. Mithra followed a rigorous rehabilitation program and adjusted her training schedule to focus on recovery. As race day approached, doubts lingered, but Ms. Mithra remained determined. With the support of her family and running community, she finished the race, not with her fastest time, but with a newfound appreciation for resilience and adaptability. Ms. Mithra's ability to overcome adversity and adapt her training demonstrated the power of determination and flexibility in the face of setbacks.

Story 2: "The Entrepreneur's Pivotal Pivot"

Mr. Lokesh, a young entrepreneur, launched a tech start-up with an innovative product idea. However, initial market feedback revealed limited interest in his original concept. Rather than being discouraged, Mr. Lokesh decided to pivot. He conducted thorough market research, listened to customer feedback, and identified an untapped niche. With resilience and adaptability, he transformed his product to meet the emerging market needs. The pivot proved to be a turning point for his startup, attracting a new customer base and leading to its eventual success. Mr. Lokesh's willingness to adapt his business strategy showcased the significance of being open to change and embracing opportunities for growth.

Story 3: "The Global Volunteer's Resilience"

Mr. Thejaswin, an enthusiastic volunteer, planned to embark on a year-long journey to assist disadvantaged communities around the world. However, unforeseen travel restrictions and budget constraints disrupted his plans. Undeterred, Mr. Thejaswin remained resilient and decided to volunteer remotely. He collaborated with local organizations, utilizing digital platforms to support community projects from afar. Though challenges arose, Mr. Thejaswin adapted his approach, staying connected with beneficiaries through virtual means. His determination to continue making a difference despite adversity showcased the importance of resilience and adaptability in pursuing impactful endeavors.

These short stories highlight the strategies of resilience and adaptability in the face of adversity. Each protagonist's ability to navigate challenges, adapt their plans, and remain determined serves as an inspiration to others, illustrating how embracing change and being resilient can lead to transformative outcomes in the pursuit of their goals.

Strategies for resilience and adaptability in the face of adversity are crucial life skills that empower individuals and communities to thrive in an ever-changing world. First and foremost, fostering a growth mindset is fundamental. Embracing challenges as opportunities for growth and viewing failures as stepping stones to success can significantly enhance one's ability to bounce back from setbacks. Cultivating this mindset not only builds resilience but also encourages the continuous pursuit of knowledge and self-improvement. Effective problem-solving skills are another key component of resilience and adaptability. The ability to analyze complex situations, identify solutions, and make informed decisions is invaluable when confronted with adversity. Problem-solving encourages a proactive rather than reactive approach to challenges, enabling individuals and communities to respond effectively to unexpected circumstances.

Moreover, social support networks play a crucial role in enhancing resilience and adaptability. Connecting with others, sharing experiences, and seeking emotional support during tough times can alleviate stress and foster a sense of belonging. Strong social bonds provide a safety net that bolsters mental and emotional well-being, ultimately enhancing one's capacity to adapt and

overcome adversity. Strategies for resilience and adaptability are vital in navigating life's inevitable challenges. Fostering a growth mindset, developing problem-solving skills, and nurturing social connections form a robust foundation for overcoming adversity and thriving in a rapidly changing world. By embracing these strategies, individuals and communities can not only weather the storms of life but also emerge from them stronger and more adaptable than ever before.

8.3. CELEBRATING SUCCESSES AND LEARNING FROM FAILURES

Story 1: "The Inventor's Journey"

Mr. Hari Krishna, an aspiring inventor, dreamed of creating a device that could provide clean and affordable energy to remote communities. After numerous failed prototypes and setbacks, Mr. Hari Krishna felt discouraged. However, with unwavering determination, he continued to learn from each failure. Through trial and error, he improved his designs, seeking advice from experts and conducting thorough research. Finally, after years of hard work, Mr. Hari Krishna developed a functional and sustainable energy device. His celebration of each successful iteration and learning from his failures not only led to his breakthrough invention but also inspired him to pursue more innovative projects, making a positive impact on the lives of many.

Story 2: "The Student's Academic Journey"

Ms. Gurunisha, a diligent student, faced challenges in her academic journey, especially in math. Despite putting in extra effort, she struggled to grasp certain concepts and earned disappointing grades. Instead of losing hope, Ms. Gurunisha sought help from her teachers and attended tutoring sessions. She celebrated her gradual improvement in understanding complex math problems and persevered through the challenges. As she continued to learn from her mistakes, Ms. Gurunisha's hard work paid off, and her math scores steadily improved. Her celebration of even the smallest achievements and commitment to learning from her failures transformed her academic journey, empowering her to excel not only in math but in other subjects as well.

Story 3: "The Social Activist's Quest"

Mr. Davis, a passionate social activist, worked tirelessly to raise awareness about environmental conservation. Despite his efforts, he faced resistance and indifference from some community members. Instead of giving up, Mr. Davis collaborated with like-minded activists and adjusted his approach to appeal to a broader audience. He celebrated the small victories, such as recruiting volunteers and organizing successful events, while also learning from the challenges he encountered. His resilience and ability to learn from failures turned his grassroots movement into a powerful force for change, inspiring others to join the cause and leading to significant policy changes in favor of environmental protection.

These short stories exemplify the importance of celebrating successes and learning from failures. Whether in the pursuit of innovation, academics, or social change, acknowledging achievements and embracing lessons from setbacks empowers individuals to persist in their endeavors and ultimately achieve their goals.

Celebrating successes and learning from failures are two intertwined facets of personal and collective growth. In the tapestry of life, these experiences form the threads that weave our journey toward self-improvement and achievement. Celebrating successes, whether big or small, fuels motivation, fosters a sense of accomplishment, and bolsters self-esteem. It provides the much-needed recognition of our efforts and acts as a beacon, guiding us toward our goals. However, it's the lessons learned from failures that truly shape us. These setbacks, disappointments, and obstacles are not roadblocks but stepping stones to resilience and wisdom. They teach us perseverance, resilience, and the art of adaptation. When we embrace both success and failure as essential teachers, we embark on a transformative journey of self-discovery and progress. It's through this dynamic interplay that we unlock our full potential, striving not only to celebrate our triumphs but also to cherish the invaluable wisdom gained through the trials and tribulations of life. This balanced approach to success and failure fosters a growth mindset, enabling us to see every experience, whether positive or negative, as an opportunity for growth. It allows us to view challenges as invitations to stretch beyond our comfort zones, innovate, and discover new capacities within ourselves.

Celebrating successes and learning from failures is not only an individual endeavor but also a communal one. In a supportive community, the celebration of achievements becomes a shared joy, amplifying the positivity and reinforcing the belief that progress is possible. Likewise, within a community, the acknowledgment of failures becomes a collective call to action, an opportunity to rally together and support one another in the face of adversity. It creates an environment where individuals feel safe to take risks, knowing that their community will stand by them, no matter the outcome. This communal approach to success and failure not only strengthens the bonds within a group but also propels the collective toward greater heights of achievement. In the grand tapestry of human existence, the threads of success and failure are woven together to create a narrative of growth, resilience, and progress. They are the yin and yang of life, two sides of the same coin that shape us into the individuals and communities we are meant to be. So, let us celebrate our successes with gratitude and humility, acknowledging the hard work and determination that brought us here. And let us embrace our failures with open hearts and inquisitive minds, knowing that within them lie the seeds of our future successes. Through this balanced dance of celebration and reflection, we not only honor our individual journeys but also contribute to the collective tapestry of human potential and possibility.

8.4. SUSTAINING MOMENTUM FOR LONG-TERM IMPACT

Story 1: "The Community Garden"

In a small neighborhood, a group of residents came together to create a community garden. They planted fruits, vegetables, and flowers to beautify the area and provide fresh produce to those in need. At first, the garden was a source of excitement and engagement, but over time, interest waned, and maintenance became challenging. Recognizing the need to sustain momentum, the organizers held workshops and educational sessions, teaching others about gardening and its benefits. They also organized regular community events, encouraging more people to get involved. With renewed enthusiasm, the garden flourished, becoming a symbol of unity and sustainability in the neighborhood, and leaving a long-term positive impact on the community's well-being.

Story 2: "The Youth Empowerment Program"

A group of passionate educators started a youth empowerment program to support at-risk teenagers in their community. The program provided mentorship, life skills training, and academic support to help young individuals overcome challenges and reach their potential. To ensure the program's long-term impact, the organizers collaborated with local businesses and community leaders to secure funding and resources. They also created a strong alumni network, enabling graduates to mentor new participants and give back to the program. As years passed, the program continued to thrive, transforming the lives of countless teenagers and instilling a sense of purpose and determination within them.

Story 3: "The Environmental Initiative"

A group of environmental enthusiasts launched an initiative to combat plastic pollution in their city. They organized regular clean-up events, conducted educational campaigns, and advocated for sustainable policies. As initial excitement waned, the organizers remained committed to sustaining momentum. They engaged with local schools, involving students in the cause and inspiring future environmental stewards. They also formed partnerships with businesses and local government, leading to the adoption of plastic-reduction measures. Through their persistent efforts, the initiative not only reduced plastic waste but also sparked a broader movement for environmental conservation in the city, leaving a lasting impact on the community and its commitment to sustainability.

These short stories exemplify the importance of sustaining momentum for long-term impact. Whether it's through community projects, empowerment programs, or environmental initiatives, the dedication to engaging, educating, and collaborating with others ensures that positive change endures and makes a lasting difference in the lives of individuals and communities alike.

Sustaining momentum for long-term impact is a critical factor in the success of any initiative, whether it be a social project, environmental conservation effort, or personal goal. It involves consistent dedication, determination, and adaptability to navigate through challenges and continue making progress over time. Often, the initial enthusiasm and excitement that accompany the start of a project may diminish as obstacles arise or the novelty wears off. However, by cultivating a culture of resilience and commitment, individuals and organizations can ensure that their efforts endure and create lasting change. One essential aspect of sustaining momentum is to maintain focus on the ultimate goal while being flexible in approach. As circumstances evolve, it is essential to adjust strategies and tactics to meet the changing needs and dynamics of the situation. Building strong partnerships and engaging with stakeholders are equally crucial in maintaining

momentum. Collaborating with like-minded individuals and organizations not only strengthens the effort but also opens up new opportunities and resources for sustainable growth.

Moreover, celebrating successes, no matter how small, plays a pivotal role in sustaining momentum. Recognizing achievements, acknowledging progress, and expressing gratitude to all those involved boosts morale and reinforces the commitment to the cause. It also provides motivation to continue striving for greater impact. Sustaining momentum for long-term impact requires a combination of perseverance, adaptability, collaboration, and celebration. By fostering a culture of dedication and learning from challenges, individuals and organizations can create a ripple effect of positive change that extends far beyond the initial efforts, leaving a lasting and meaningful impact on the communities and causes they serve.